Haunted House

Aunt Helen turned another sharp corner and jerked the old car to a stop in front of the huge, old inn. "So," she prompted, "what do you think?"

No one said a word. Before them in the dim twilight sat a large, ramshackle building. The yard was overgrown with weeds and bushes, and the porch was sagging in the middle. Shutters hung at odd angles, and the paint was peeling.

But Elizabeth didn't dwell on any of those things. Her eyes were drawn to the bell tower at the very top of the inn. The black bell hung motionless, vividly outlined against the deep red sky.

Aunt Helen chuckled. "There are some wonderful stories about this inn," she said. "Why, some people even say that the place is haunted!"

"Haunted!" Jessica repeated nervously, while Elizabeth stood silent, her eyes fixed on the creepy bell tower.

SWEET VALLEY TWINS titles, published by Bantam Books. Ask your bookseller for titles you have missed:

SWEET VALLEY TWINS

◇ SUPER CHILLER ◇

The Ghost in the Bell Tower

Written by
Jamie Suzanne

Created by
FRANCINE PASCAL

A BANTAM BOOK
NEW YORK · TORONTO · LONDON · SYDNEY · AUCKLAND

THE GHOST IN THE BELL TOWER

A BANTAM BOOK 0 553 40466 0

Originally published in U.S.A. by Bantam Skylark Books

First publication in Great Britain

PRINTING HISTORY
Bantam edition published 1992
Sweet Valley High® and Sweet Valley Twins are registered
trademarks of Francine Pascal.

Conceived by Francine Pascal.

Produced by Daniel Weiss Associates, Inc., 33 West 17th Street, New
York, NY 10011

All rights reserves.

Bantam Books are published by Transworld Publishers Ltd.,
61–63 Uxbridge Road, Ealing, London W5 5SA,
in Australia by Transworld Publishers (Australia) Pty. Ltd.,
15–23 Helles Avenue, Moorebank, NSW 2170, and in New
Zealand by Transworld Publishers (N.Z.) Ltd.,
3 William Pickering Drive, Albany, Auckland.

Made and printed in Great Britain by
BPCC Hazells Ltd
Member of BPCC Ltd

To Katherine Applegate

One

◇

"Run, before it's too late!" Jessica Wakefield screamed as she leapt out of her chair.

Her twin sister rolled her eyes. "Jess, it's only a *movie*," Elizabeth said, exasperated.

"Yeah, Jessica," Steven, the twins' fourteen-year-old brother, added. "Get a grip on yourself, will you?"

A commercial flickered on and Jessica sank back into her chair. "I just *love* scary movies!"

Elizabeth, lying on the floor near the TV, rolled onto her back and looked at her twin. "You could have fooled me," she remarked. "You were screaming so loudly, I thought I was going to go deaf!"

"Speaking of going deaf, would you mind turning down the TV a little, Elizabeth?" Joe

Howell asked. Joe, a good friend of Steven's, was spending the night at the Wakefields' house.

"Sure, Joe." Elizabeth lowered the volume and turned back to Jessica. "To tell you the truth, Jess, I don't think this movie's nearly as scary as the Amanda Howard mystery I just finished reading."

"Why would you want to read a mystery when watching one is so much more fun?" Jessica responded.

Elizabeth groaned. She was used to disagreeing with her twin. But sometimes it still surprised her that they could look so much alike yet have such different personalities. Both Elizabeth and Jessica had long, shiny blond hair and blue-green eyes. They were identical, right down to the tiny dimple in their left cheeks.

But their personalities made it easy to tell the twins apart. Elizabeth was the more serious, responsible twin. She was a good student and loved school. Since she hoped to become a writer someday, Elizabeth was especially proud of her position as the editor of the *Sweet Valley Sixers*, the sixth-grade newspaper she had helped found. She was logical and down-to-earth, the kind of friend who could always be counted on to help solve a problem or lend a sympathetic ear.

Jessica, on the other hand, was spontaneous and fun-loving, and she enjoyed being the center of attention. Jessica was a member of the Unicorn Club, a group of the prettiest and most popular girls at Sweet Valley Middle School. Elizabeth thought the Unicorns were silly—they spent all their time talking about boys, clothing, and soap operas. Jessica, on the other hand, thought Elizabeth's friends, who preferred books to boys, were boring.

But in spite of their differences, the girls were best friends. They shared a special bond that only twins could have. No matter what problem they faced, they knew they could always put their heads together and come up with a solution.

"Don't you think the guy who got killed by the ghost was adorable?" Jessica asked Elizabeth.

"Shh!" Steven hissed as he checked his watch. "The movie's back!"

"Maybe we should turn the lights back on," Jessica whispered. "In case it gets too creepy."

"Hey, some of us are trying to watch!" Steven snapped.

Jessica glared at her brother and turned her attention back to the movie. The heroine was searching a haunted house for her missing cat. A hideous ghost was following close behind her. Suddenly she came face-to-face with the horrible image of a zombie. A low, terrifying moan filled the air. Jessica screamed.

"Quiet!" Steven commanded, sitting bolt upright. "What's that noise?"

The strange moaning continued, even though the zombie was no longer on the television screen.

"I hear it, too," Elizabeth said.

"It's *here!*" Jessica shrieked. She jumped to her feet, her eyes darting frantically around the dark den. "The noise is coming from somewhere in this house!"

"I think Jessica's right, Steven," Joe said nervously.

The noise came again, and the strange wail seemed to fill the entire house.

"We've got to get out of here!" Jessica cried. She reached for Elizabeth's arm and tried to pull her to her feet.

But Elizabeth wouldn't budge. She clicked off the TV with the remote control and glanced up at the ceiling. At last the wailing stopped.

"Jess is right, Elizabeth," Steven agreed. "We'd better get out of here before it's too late."

Elizabeth smiled. "You mean before we figure out your little trick, don't you, Steven?"

"What do you mean, trick?" Steven asked innocently.

"Give it up, Steven," Elizabeth replied. "I'll give you credit, though. You almost had me fooled for a minute."

Jessica glanced at Steven and Joe, who were exchanging guilty smiles. "Oh, *I* get it," she said, a smile dawning on her face. "You almost had *me* fooled, too."

"We *did* fool you, Jess!" Steven laughed. "You were ready to run for your life!"

"I was not!" Jessica retorted defiantly.

"Then how did you know we were tricking you?" Steven asked.

"That's simple." Jessica paused and knitted her brows. "I had a feeling you guys were up to something, because Joe's a notorious practical joker. Everyone knows that."

"*Sure* you did," Steven responded skeptically.

"C'mon, it was so obvious!" Elizabeth added. "I saw you rummaging through the junk drawer in the kitchen for some batteries, Steven, so I knew you were planning to use something battery-powered. Then Joe asked me to turn down the sound on the TV, and you kept checking your watch. And when the noise seemed to be coming from the air-conditioning ducts in the ceiling, it hit me. You two recorded the moaning on Steven's portable tape player earlier today, then you put the tape recorder near an air-conditioning duct upstairs so the sound would travel through the house, but be hard to track down."

"But they were with us when the noise started," Jessica pointed out. "How could Steven and Joe have started the tape?"

Elizabeth grinned. "That's easy. They left the first part of their tape blank and recorded Joe's wailing after a few minutes. The tape could have played for a while before it reached the recorded noises. Remember when Steven went to the kitchen to get a drink? He could have sneaked upstairs without our noticing. Am I right, Steven?"

Steven frowned. "You're no fun to trick, Elizabeth. You're too logical."

"And you guys are too sick," Jessica snapped.

"We were just trying to liven up your summer vacation," Joe said sweetly.

"How very thoughtful." Jessica reached for the remote control in Elizabeth's hand and turned the TV back on. The movie was already over. "Now we'll never know what happened to the girl!"

"I can guess what happened," Elizabeth said. "It's pretty obvious, if you just think about it for a minute—"

"Thanks anyway," Jessica snapped. "But I'll wait until the movie is rerun." She flopped into the chair. "You know, not everything has a logical explanation, Elizabeth. One of these days you're going to run into something that can't be explained."

"I still can't believe Jessica fell for our practical joke last night!" Steven said the next morning.

Elizabeth looked up from her toast and shook her head. "I'm sure she would have figured it out," she remarked. *"Eventually!"*

Elizabeth and Steven were still laughing when Jessica entered the kitchen carrying a handful of mail.

"What's so funny?" she asked.

"You, last night!" Steven answered.

"I hate it when you and Joe Howell get together," Jessica said. "You're bad enough all by yourself, Steven."

"Any mail for us?" Elizabeth asked.

Jessica shook her head. "I was hoping for a postcard from Ellen Riteman. She's in Florida visiting her grandparents." She paused and examined a long white envelope. "This is addressed to Steven, Elizabeth, and Jessica Wakefield! I wonder who it's from?"

"Check the return address," Elizabeth suggested.

Jessica read the upper-left-hand corner of the envelope. "All it says is 'The Lakeview Inn, Holton, California.' Who could that be?" She ripped open the envelope.

Steven reached for his third doughnut. "Why do you get to open it? My name came first!"

"Because *I* got the mail while you sat here in the kitchen feeding your face," Jessica answered. She pulled out a piece of heavy white stationery and unfolded it. Jessica skipped to the signature at the bottom of the page. "It's from Aunt Helen!"

Aunt Helen, who was actually the twins' great-aunt, was one of Jessica and Elizabeth's favorite relatives.

"Aunt Helen!" Elizabeth repeated. "Let me see." She ran over to get a better look.

"What's that?" Mrs. Wakefield asked as she came into the kitchen.

"A letter from Aunt Helen!" Elizabeth answered.

Mrs. Wakefield smiled. "What a surprise! Why don't you read it out loud, Jessica?"

Jessica cleared her throat and began to read.

My dears,

I am writing you with some surprising and wonderful news. It seems that your great-aunt is now the proud owner of a 15-room inn in northern California. An old friend left it to me in her will—quite unexpectedly—and I have decided to reopen the inn once I have restored it to its original beauty.

I am writing to invite you kids to help me with the renovations. It won't be easy. The place is a mess and it's covered with cobwebs and dust. But it sits on a crystal-clear lake surrounded by hundred-foot pines, and there is plenty to explore. I have also invited your cousins Stacey and Robin.

Once the renovations are complete, I look forward to holding a family reunion at the inn.

I do hope you'll take me up on my invitation.
I'm sure we'll have a wonderful time!

Much love,
Aunt Helen

Jessica put down the letter, and a broad grin spread across her face. "Elizabeth, can you believe it? Just when we were afraid this summer vacation was going to be the most boring one in history, Aunt Helen saves the day!" She looked at Mrs. Wakefield. "We *can* go, can't we, Mom?"

"Of course you can. You know, Aunt Helen's had some heart problems lately. I'd feel a lot better knowing you were there helping her out with such a big project. Still, I hope she's not taking on more than she can handle."

"Not with *us* there to help," Elizabeth said happily. "And Robin and Stacey will be there, too! We'll have so much fun, Jess!"

"Four girls against one guy?" Steven interrupted. "That doesn't sound like fun to me."

Mrs. Wakefield smiled. "Maybe we can talk Aunt Helen into allowing you to bring a friend along, Steven. Then you won't be so outnumbered."

"All right! Joe and I will have a ball!"

"Joe Howell?" Jessica whined. "Anyone but Joe, please!"

"I'm sure Joe and Steven will be on their best behavior, Jess," Mrs. Wakefield reassured her. "They might just surprise you."

Elizabeth winked at Jessica. "That's what we're afraid of!"

Jessica shrugged and sighed. "Come on, Elizabeth," she said. "We've got better things to worry about than *those* two. Let's go upstairs and start packing!"

Two

◇

Jessica glanced at the mound of clothing on her bed and groaned. "I've been packing since yesterday and I'm *still* not done!"

"Why don't you just pack everything, to be on the safe side?" Lila Fowler suggested. Lila and Janet Howell, fellow members of the Unicorn Club, sat on Jessica's bedroom floor, watching her prepare for her big trip.

"Even though you're going to be out of town, you'll still be required to wear purple every day," Janet reminded Jessica. "It's part of the official Unicorn regulations, you know." Janet, an eighth grader and Joe's sister, was the president of the Unicorns.

"I will," Jessica said seriously. She reached for a sock Lila had discovered. "I've been looking for that for months! Where'd you find it?"

"Under your bed," Lila replied. "Want me to see what else is under there?"

"Not unless you have a strong stomach!"

Jessica spun around to see Steven and Joe standing in the hallway outside her door. "You're one to talk, Steven," she snapped. "I wouldn't go in *your* room without a gas mask!"

Steven pretended to be hurt. "And here I went to all the trouble of bringing you that extra suitcase from the attic!"

Jessica softened instantly. "Great! I was running out of room."

"Aren't you going to thank your big brother?" Joe prompted.

"Thanks, Steven," Jessica said, grabbing the suitcase.

"Any time, Jess," Steven replied, grinning broadly.

"Your brother has the *cutest* smile," Janet gushed as soon as the boys were out of earshot.

Jessica rolled her eyes. "You ought to try living with him for a day!"

"He couldn't be any worse than Joe," Janet said as she reached for a magazine on Jessica's desk. "If Joe plays one more practical joke on me, I swear I'm going to make my parents put him up for adoption."

Jessica cleared a place on her bed for the empty suitcase. "I was hoping Aunt Helen would say Steven couldn't bring any guests," she admitted. "But when my parents called her last night, she said yes."

"Here's the last load from the dryer, Jess," Elizabeth announced as she came into the room. "Not that you need them!"

"How many suitcases did *you* pack, Elizabeth?" Lila asked.

"Just one," Elizabeth replied. "I've got a little bit of room left over, Jessica, if you need it."

Jessica lifted the big suitcase Steven had brought her onto the bed. "Thanks, Elizabeth," she said as she flipped open the brass locks and lifted the top, "but there should be plenty of room in—" Jessica stopped and let out an earsplitting scream.

"Jess! What is it?"

Jessica pointed a trembling finger at the open suitcase.

"It's a *hand!*" Lila shrieked. "A human hand!"

"Gross!" Jessica backed toward the wall. "There's blood!"

Janet's face was pale, but she peered a little more closely at the severed hand. "Are you sure it's real?" she asked anxiously.

While the others watched in horror, Elizabeth stepped forward confidently and picked up the bloody limb. "Of *course* it's not real," she told them. "It's plastic. Another Steven and Joe prank," she said, tossing the hand to Jessica, who let it drop to the floor. "You should have been suspicious the moment Steven volunteered to get that suitcase from the attic, Jess."

"I'm not the only one who fell for it," Jessica retorted. "Janet did, too, and she's seen a million of Joe's juvenile tricks!"

Elizabeth smiled and tapped her index finger on her temple. "It's like I keep telling you, Jess. Everything has a logical explanation, if you just use your brain."

Jessica shook her head as Elizabeth left the room. "One of these days I'm going to teach that Ms. Know-it-all a lesson."

"Now, don't forget to call us when you get to Aunt Helen's," Mrs. Wakefield told the twins as they prepared to board the bus early the next morning.

"We will, Mom," Elizabeth promised.

"And remember, your aunt has had some heart trouble," Mr. Wakefield added, looking sternly at Joe and Steven. "Be sure to help her out all you can. And do the twins a favor, huh, guys? No more practical jokes."

"Sure, Dad," Steven agreed.

Jessica smiled triumphantly and noted the disappointed look on Steven's face.

After hugging their parents good-bye, the

twins settled in seats near the rear of the bus. "How long will this trip take, anyway?" Jessica asked.

"We won't arrive until early evening," Elizabeth informed her. "So I came prepared with my new Amanda Howard mystery to read and two bologna sandwiches—one for each of us."

"I planned ahead, too," Jessica boasted, reaching for her backpack. She pulled out the new issue of *SMASH!* magazine and two big bags of chocolate-chip cookies. "One for each of us," she said with a sly smile.

"Aren't we there yet?" Jessica asked, much later. "It's almost dark!"

"I just saw a sign that said Holton is four miles away," Elizabeth answered. She looked out the window again and watched a huge tree whiz past in a dark green blur.

At last the bus slowed and turned onto a small road. An old wooden sign welcomed them to Holton, California, population 1,217. "It's awfully tiny compared to Sweet Valley," Jessica noted as the bus lumbered through the center of town. "I don't even see a mall."

"It looks like that general store on the corner is the closest you're going to get to a mall," Elizabeth said with a giggle.

"How boring! And everything's so run down! I hope the inn isn't this gross."

"Aunt Helen warned us that the inn was in bad shape," Elizabeth reminded her twin. "That's why we're here, remember?"

"Hey! I see Aunt Helen waiting outside the bus station!" Jessica cried, her nose pressed to the window. "And there's Robin and Stacey! Robin's changed her hairstyle again! She looks *so* sophisticated."

The twins' cousins lived in San Diego, and Jessica and Elizabeth didn't get to see them as often as they would have liked. Robin was just a few months younger than the twins, and whenever the three of them got together they acted more like triplets than cousins. In fact, with her blond shoulder-length hair and blue eyes, Robin looked a lot like the twins. Robin's little sister, Stacey, was eight and she had bright red hair and lots of freckles.

Jessica and Elizabeth were the first ones off the bus. While Elizabeth gave her great-aunt a long hug, Jessica ran to greet Robin and Stacey.

"When did you guys get here?"

"About an hour ago," Robin answered. "We took an express bus from San Diego."

"I hardly recognized them when they got off the bus," Aunt Helen said, walking over to greet Jessica. "Or you, either. You all look so grown-up!"

"You haven't changed a bit, Aunt Helen," Jessica said.

Aunt Helen smiled, her clear blue eyes twinkling.

"Hi, Aunt Helen!" Steven called as he and Joe got off the bus.

"Why, I never!" Aunt Helen exclaimed. "If I didn't know better, I'd swear you were your father, Steven Wakefield! You've shot up like a beanstalk! How'd you get to be so tall?"

"He eats twenty-four hours a day," Jessica answered. "I hope your refrigerator is well stocked!"

"This is my friend, Joe Howell," Steven said.

"Welcome, Joe," Aunt Helen said, shaking his hand. "I'm so glad you decided to come along. We're going to need all the help we can get!"

"These are my cousins, Robin and Stacey," Steven told Joe.

"Watch out for Joe," Jessica advised. "He's the world's most obnoxious practical joker."

"Jessica's just mad because she falls for everything," Steven teased. "Tell them about the severed hand, Jess."

"The *what*?" Stacey cried.

"Never mind," Jessica said. Elizabeth saw her twin's cheeks redden.

"Don't worry, Stacey," Elizabeth reassured

her cousin. "I always figure out what they're up to."

"Ms. Computer Brain *never* gets tricked," Jessica said, sounding annoyed.

"Well, shall we get going?" Aunt Helen asked. "I can't wait for you to see the inn! And I'll bet you kids are starving after such a long trip."

Aunt Helen's car was an old black limousine, so old that it looked to the kids like it belonged in a museum. "I inherited this car with the inn," she explained as the engine growled to a start. As the car jerked forward Aunt Helen glanced back at her passengers. "So, what do you think of beautiful downtown Holton?"

The twins looked at Robin and Stacey helplessly. When no one answered, Aunt Helen spoke up. "I know, I know. It's a little rustic. I haven't been here in years myself. But I used to come to Holton with my family when I was a young girl. We had a cabin north of town. Way back in the 1800s Holton was a gold-mining town, you know."

"Do you think there's still gold here?" Steven asked excitedly.

"Most of the mines dried up long ago," Aunt Helen told him. "Still," she added with a smile, "you never know what you might find if you look hard enough."

The car veered around a corner onto a narrow

dirt road. Huge trees formed a dark canopy over the road, blotting out the last red rays of sunset.

"It's a shame you arrived just as it's getting dark," Aunt Helen commented. "I'm afraid you're not going to get a very favorable impression of the inn. You must remember it's been abandoned for almost seventy years. But back in its heyday it was a very busy gambling parlor and hotel, and with a little work I'm sure we can restore it to its original beauty."

She turned another sharp corner and jerked the old car to a stop. "So," she prompted. "What do you think?"

No one said a word. Before them in the dim twilight sat a huge, ramshackle building. The yard was overgrown with weeds and bushes, and the porch was sagging in the middle. Shutters hung at odd angles, and the paint was peeling and blistering.

But Elizabeth didn't dwell on any of those things. Her eyes were drawn to the bell tower at the very top of the inn. The black bell hung motionless, vividly outlined against the deep red sky.

"I know it needs a lot of work," Aunt Helen said, "but don't you think it has potential?"

"Sure it does, Aunt Helen," Jessica reassured her.

"A little paint, a little weeding, and it'll be as good as new," Steven added.

"You know, there are some wonderful stories about this inn." Aunt Helen chuckled. "Why, some people even say the place is haunted!"

"Haunted?" Stacey echoed nervously.

"I'm sure he's a friendly ghost, dear," Aunt Helen said kindly.

The children jumped out of the car and gathered their bags. Only Elizabeth remained in the car, her eyes fixed on the old bell tower.

"Elizabeth? Are you coming, dear?"

Elizabeth looked back to see Aunt Helen peering through the car window. "Oh, yes. I was just looking at that bell tower. There's something about it. . . ." She didn't want to admit that the tower gave her the creeps.

"Charming, isn't it?"

Elizabeth nodded and climbed out of the car. *Charming* was definitely not the word she had in mind.

Three

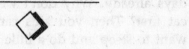

Jessica and Robin were the first ones inside the inn. Robin pulled open a heavy, creaky door and the girls entered a huge room lit only by the pale remains of twilight. All the furnishings were draped with dust-covered sheets, and cobwebs hung from the ceilings.

"It looks like something out of a movie," Robin whispered.

"Yeah. A *horror* movie!" Jessica whispered back.

Aunt Helen came in with the others. She made her way past some crates to a floor lamp covered with a fringed shade and clicked it on. Soft yellow light filled the room. "As you can see, there's still a lot of cleaning to be done," she said, brushing a cobweb off the shade.

"It *is* a little dusty," Jessica agreed.

"That's seventy years' worth of dust, my dear," Aunt Helen observed wryly.

"Where do we sleep?" Steven asked.

"Oh, don't worry," Aunt Helen assured him. "Several of the upstairs bedrooms have already been cleaned, as well as the kitchen and dining room. I've had a crew of workers here for several days already. Why don't we have something to eat first? Then you kids can decide where you want to sleep and do a little exploring."

A few minutes later they were all sitting in the dining room enjoying sandwiches and home-made berry pie.

"This table could seat a zillion people!" Stacey exclaimed, looking at the long row of empty seats beside her.

"Twenty, to be exact. There are fifteen bedrooms upstairs, and a huge attic on the top floor," Aunt Helen said as she cut another slice of pie for Steven. "That's where the entrance to the bell tower is located, although it's blocked off with boxes and furniture right now."

Elizabeth shuddered. She had no desire to go anywhere near that tower.

"I thought you girls could start by cleaning up the attic. There are too many stairs for me to tackle," Aunt Helen added. "And there's an old boathouse out by the lake that I thought Steven and Joe could work on." She smiled gratefully. "I can't tell you how much it means to me to have you all here like this. Sometimes I have my doubts about reopening this old place. It really will help to have my family around for moral support."

"Who was the person who left you the inn, Aunt Helen?" Elizabeth asked.

Aunt Helen smiled wistfully. "A wonderful old woman named Alexandra Whyte. She was a neighbor of mine for years when I lived in San Francisco. I used to visit her every day and bring her flowers from my garden, and sometimes we'd talk about her childhood. She would tell me about the inn, which had been in her family since the turn of the century. She was born here, in fact. But it closed down when she was still a young woman, and she had never been back since." Aunt Helen took a sip of coffee before continuing. "Anyway, when she passed away, no one was more surprised than I when Alexandra's lawyer informed me she had willed The Lakeview Inn to me! She had never married, and I suppose I was the closest thing she had to family. Of course, I had no intention of fixing up the place—that is, until I drove out to take a look at it. I had seen it before, you know, when I was a little girl. But I hadn't remembered it too clearly. When I saw it again after all those years, I just fell in love with it!"

Elizabeth glanced at Jessica. It was a little

hard to understand why Aunt Helen had fallen in love with such a decrepit old place!

Aunt Helen caught Elizabeth's look and laughed. "I know what you're thinking. You're afraid your old aunt has gone stark raving mad!"

Elizabeth giggled. "It's just that it's still a little bit, uh, *dusty*. But it has lots of potential—"

"It's got more than potential," Aunt Helen replied, a gleam in her eye. "Why, The Lakeview Inn has its very own ghost, for goodness' sake! How many places can make that claim?"

"Is it really true?" Stacey asked.

Aunt Helen shrugged. "That's what the locals tell me. They say it's been haunted by the same ghost for seventy years." She winked at Stacey. "So far he's been very polite. I haven't heard a peep out of him."

"You don't really believe those stories, do you, Aunt Helen?" Elizabeth asked doubtfully.

Aunt Helen began to gather the dishes. "Oh, I don't know. I sort of *like* the idea of having my very own ghost. It makes the inn special." She patted Stacey's head affectionately. "Who knows? Maybe I should mention the ghost in our advertisements. It might do wonders for business!"

"You aren't serious!" Elizabeth cried.

"Elizabeth's far too *logical* to believe in ghosts," Jessica explained snidely.

"You can't rely on logic to explain everything," Aunt Helen replied.

"That's what *I* keep telling her," Jessica said. "One of these days she'll see I'm right."

Elizabeth sighed and pushed back her chair. She was tired of arguing with her twin about ghosts and logic.

"Do you need some help with the dishes, Aunt Helen?" Elizabeth asked.

"That would be lovely, dear."

"I think Joe and I will check out the boathouse, if that's OK with you, Aunt Helen," Steven said.

"Of course. Just don't be too long."

The boys grabbed some flashlights and ran off.

"Are you coming, Jess?" Elizabeth asked as she gathered some dishes.

"We'll help tomorrow night," Jessica answered quickly. "Robin and Stacey and I are going to, um, explore a little."

Elizabeth shrugged. "Suit yourself." Jessica always had a knack for avoiding chores!

After Elizabeth had helped Aunt Helen wash the dishes, she went to find Jessica, Robin, and Stacey. She walked through the empty main room and called their names. When no one answered, she decided to go upstairs.

Elizabeth climbed the staircase. At the top of the stairs a long hallway extended in either direction. The only light came from several small wall lamps that flickered whenever she took a step.

Elizabeth peeked into the first room she came to. In the dim glow of the hall lights she could make out a few chairs, a desk, and several paintings stacked against the wall. She felt jittery, although she knew there was no logical reason to be. She was in an old inn, not a haunted house!

"Jessica?" she called. There was no answer.

Then Elizabeth heard hushed voices coming from the room at the very end of the hallway. "Jess?" she called again as she cautiously approached the room. She peeked in the doorway, and to her relief saw Robin, Stacey, and Jessica sitting on a bed.

"*There* you are!" Elizabeth exclaimed. "Why didn't you guys answer me?"

The three girls looked up in surprise. "We didn't hear you, Elizabeth," Jessica answered quickly, jumping off the bed.

"I called and called," Elizabeth insisted.

"What do you think of this room?" Robin asked. "Stacey and I are going to sleep here."

"It's great!" Elizabeth answered. The room contained a grand old fireplace, two big antique beds, a tall bookcase, and a dresser over which hung an oval mirror. Elizabeth walked over to one of the windows. "What a great view of the lake!" she added.

"I've already picked out our room," Jessica said excitedly. "It's right next door. Come see!"

The twins' room was smaller than Robin and Stacey's. It had only one window and no fireplace. But both beds boasted ornately carved headboards, and beautiful purple satin comforters, and there was a full-length mirror on one wall. Elizabeth took one look at the comforters and the mirror, and knew why her twin had chosen the room.

"I wonder who he is?" Stacey asked, pointing to a portrait of a distinguished-looking gentleman with a thick handlebar mustache.

"That's Alexandra's father," said Aunt Helen from the doorway. "Phineas Whyte." She handed Jessica a pile of towels. "There are two bathrooms on this floor," she explained. "So take your pick. Steven and Joe informed me they're taking the bedroom at the far end of the hallway."

"Good," Jessica said. "The farther away, the better!"

"I've turned one of the downstairs parlors into a bedroom," Aunt Helen continued. "That way I don't have to climb up and down stairs all the time. Be sure to let me know if there's anything else you need. And by the way, I called both sets of parents to let them know you all made it here safe and sound." Aunt Helen smiled. "I can't tell you how good it is to have you here with me! We're going to make The Lakeview Inn a very special place to visit!"

"Jess, are you asleep?" Elizabeth whispered late that night.

The only reply was the sound of her sister's steady breathing.

Elizabeth rolled over and punched her big down pillow with her fist. For some reason, she just couldn't seem to fall asleep. Perhaps it was being in a new place, or the bright moonlight spilling through the ruffled curtains. Or maybe it was the memory of that creepy tower.

Elizabeth was in the middle of counting sheep when she heard a soft tapping on the door. "Who's there?" she whispered loudly.

"It's us, Robin and Stacey," Robin hissed, pushing the door open a crack. "Please, can we come in?"

"What's wrong?" Elizabeth asked.

"Go back to sleep, Elizabeth," Jessica mumbled into her pillow. "It's the middle of the night."

"Jess, it's Robin and—" Elizabeth flicked on the lamp on her nightstand and gasped.

Robin and Stacey were each swathed in a huge blanket. Their faces were as pale as the moonlight, and their lips were tinged with blue. Both girls shivered uncontrollably.

"What's wrong with you?" Elizabeth cried. "You look as if you're freezing to death!"

"Can we sleep in here with you?" Stacey asked, her teeth chattering loudly.

"It's like a refrigerator in our room!" Robin added.

Jessica rolled over and groaned. "Please go back to sleep," she murmured. "I need my beauty rest."

"Jess, there's something wrong," Elizabeth said loudly. "Wake up."

Jessica's eyes fluttered open. "What are you guys doing here?" she asked wearily. She leaned on one elbow and blinked her eyes. "That's the ugliest lipstick I've *ever* seen," she said bluntly.

"It's not lipstick, Jessica!" Stacey cried. "Our room is ice-cold!"

Robin wrapped her blanket around her even more tightly. "Come see, you guys. You won't believe this."

By now Jessica was fully awake. "But our room is perfectly warm," she pointed out. "Why should yours be any different?"

"I'm sure there's a simple explanation," Elizabeth said.

"Put on your robes," Robin advised. "You'll need them."

When the twins stepped into their cousins'

room a moment later, they gasped. "It must be twenty below zero in here!" Jessica cried.

Elizabeth wrapped her arms around herself and shivered. "Maybe you left one of the windows open," she suggested. "The breeze coming from the lake is probably very cold at night." She walked over to a window and pulled back the curtains.

"We checked the windows," Robin said. "They're shut tight."

Elizabeth tapped her finger on her chin. "How about the fireplace flue?"

"What's that?" Stacey asked.

"It's like a little door in the chimney," Elizabeth explained. "You open it when you make a fire. If it's open, the warm air in the room could have escaped." She got down on her hands and knees and peered into the fireplace. "Nope," Elizabeth said, standing up and wiping the soot off her hands. "It's closed, too."

"Well, if it isn't an open window or an open fireplace flue that's making the room cold, then why *is* it so cold in here?" Robin demanded.

Jessica's eyes darted around the room. "Maybe . . ." she began.

"What, Jess?" Robin prompted.

"Well, I know this sounds crazy," Jessica said at last. "But I remember hearing somewhere that *ghosts* create cold spots. Maybe the inn really *is* haunted!"

Four

"Jessica, that's crazy!" Elizabeth protested. "Ghosts?"

"Don't forget what Aunt Helen told us. Lots of people say this inn is haunted," Robin reminded Elizabeth.

Stacey reached for her sister's hand. "Please don't make me sleep here tonight," she begged.

Elizabeth scanned the room for a possible clue. "Maybe the radiator isn't working," she suggested. "This place *is* old, after all." She walked over to the radiator and felt it. It was pinging loudly, and was warm to the touch.

"That's weird," she said. "How could the room be this cold when the heat's working?"

"I'll tell you how!" Robin blurted as she ran for the door. "This room is haunted!"

"Calm down, Robin," Elizabeth said, but

Robin and Stacey were already in the hallway. "I can't believe they're acting this way!"

Jessica put her finger to her lips. "Just in case there *is* a ghost, I'd watch what I say if I were you, Elizabeth," she advised. "If he hears you talking that way, he may just decide to teach you a lesson!"

"How'd you sleep last night, Robin?" Elizabeth asked the next morning. Robin had shared Jessica's bed, and Stacey had crawled in with Elizabeth.

Robin put down her lip gloss and sighed. "How do you *think* I slept, knowing my bedroom might be haunted?"

Jessica leaned against the doorframe and stretched her arms high overhead. "Morning," she said. "Any more sign of the ghost?"

Robin shook her head. "No."

"Maybe he haunts only one room of the house," Jessica suggested. "Ghosts can be very picky."

"Since when are you the resident ghost expert?" Elizabeth asked.

"I've watched every horror movie there is!" Jessica said indignantly.

"Well, so have I," Elizabeth replied calmly. "But the difference between us is that *I* realize those movies are fake."

"Kids! Breakfast is on the table!" Aunt Helen called from downstairs.

"I wonder if we should tell Aunt Helen about what happened last night?" Robin asked as she applied a bit of blue eyeshadow to her lids.

"No," Elizabeth said firmly. "Mom and Dad told us Aunt Helen has had heart trouble. The last thing we want to do is upset her. There has to be a logical explanation for what happened. Let's not jump to conclusions."

"I hate to admit it, Robin," Jessica conceded at last, "but Elizabeth is usually right about these things."

"Don't you mean I'm *always* right?" Elizabeth said with a grin.

Jessica groaned. "There probably *is* a logical explanation, Robin."

"That's more like it!" Elizabeth exclaimed.

"Still, you should watch what you say about the ghost," Jessica added in a loud whisper. "Just in case he's eavesdropping."

The three girls woke Stacey and headed down the long hallway. They were almost to the stairway when the door to one of the empty bedrooms flew open.

Two figures, draped in white sheets, leapt into the hallway.

Jessica made a show of yawning. "Breakfast is ready, boys," she said nonchalantly.

"How juvenile," Stacey remarked loudly.

"Don't you get it?" Joe asked, tagging along behind them and stumbling over his sheet. "We're the ghosts of The Lakeview Inn!"

"I wish *these* ghosts were all we had to worry about," Elizabeth muttered.

After a breakfast of blueberry pancakes and fresh orange juice, the kids set off to begin their work on the inn. Already a crew of workers was busy outside, hammering and sawing and painting.

Steven and Joe headed down to the boathouse, and Aunt Helen gave the girls instructions on the work they were to do in the attic.

"That attic is wall-to-wall junk," she explained. "And your job is to sort through it. Keep what you think is important and set the rest aside. We'll throw it away or give it to charity. And there's a big pile of odds and ends blocking the entrance to the bell tower at the back of the attic. Our main goal is to clear a path so that the workmen can check the tower to see if it's structurally sound. Who knows what shape it's in after seventy years?"

Once again Elizabeth felt the slight uneasiness she'd felt when she first saw the bell tower.

"I think it sounds like fun!" Robin exclaimed. "I love digging through old stuff."

"There are plenty of treasures up there,"

Aunt Helen assured them. "The whole history of the inn, if you look hard enough!"

The attic could be reached only by a steep staircase that folded out of the second-story ceiling. Elizabeth stood on a chair and pulled it down.

The four girls climbed cautiously up the stairs. The attic was huge and dark and smelled of mildew and mothballs. Small, dusty windows lined the low walls. The light shining through them was as pale as candlelight.

"Aren't there any electric lights up here?" Jessica asked, climbing the last step.

"Aunt Helen said there's a bulb hanging from the ceiling," Elizabeth pointed out. "The pull-chain should be right over the top of the stairs."

Jessica reached up blindly in the dark and found the chain. She pulled it and a dim light came on.

"Gross," Stacey said as she climbed up beside the other girls and looked around. "I think it looked better in the dark."

"Aunt Helen wasn't kidding. It *is* a mess up here!" Robin moaned.

The four girls stood in the middle of the attic and surveyed the chaos. Piles of musty old books, trunks of every shape and size, and cardboard boxes brimming with odds and ends filled the space. Clothes hung on a long rack against one wall, and an odd assortment of mismatched china filled an antique cupboard. A moth-eaten wicker mannequin stood at attention in a corner. A broad-brimmed hat decorated with faded flowers sat on its head.

"Where do we start?" Jessica asked. She turned to her sister, but Elizabeth was staring fixedly at a little door at the back of the attic. It was barely visible behind towering piles of cardboard boxes.

"Elizabeth," Jessica said again.

"That must be the door that leads to the bell tower," Elizabeth said slowly.

"So?"

"So—nothing. It's just that when I first saw it, I thought it looked pretty creepy. I mean, in an interesting sort of way," Elizabeth added hastily.

"This whole *place* looks pretty creepy," Stacey said.

"Aunt Helen said the bell was rung to signal the hours for the miners who worked in the area," Robin said.

"Still, there's something so lonely and abandoned about the tower," Elizabeth said quietly. She shook her head and tried to break free of the uneasy feeling that had passed over her. "Anyway, I guess we should get to work. I'll start by cleaning out the corner with all the books."

"I want to sort through the old clothing!" Jessica said.

For the next two hours the girls worked steadily. Jessica, Robin, and Stacey spent as much time trying on old clothes as they did actually cleaning up, but Elizabeth was too busy to notice. She was enjoying sorting through the piles of dusty, leather-bound books; it was like stepping back into the past. Every so often she would set one aside to look at later.

Elizabeth had sorted through the first pile when she came upon a heavy book covered in faded blue satin. "Hey, you guys!" she called. "You'll never guess what I've found. It's a photo album!"

"Show us later," Jessica called back. "We're trying on these great hats!"

Elizabeth set the album aside with the other special books. And then she made an even more exciting discovery. She found a small black leather book with the words *My Diary* embossed on the cover in gold script.

Gently, Elizabeth opened to the first page. The paper was thin and yellowed with age, but the handwriting was youthful and flowing. *Alexandra Whyte*, it said. *August, 1919.*

It was Alexandra's diary!

Just as she opened her mouth to tell the others of her newest find, Steven's excited voice filled the attic.

"Hey, you guys," he called from the stairs. "You'll never guess what Joe and I discovered!"

"I thought you were cleaning the boathouse!" Jessica scolded, her hands on her hips.

Steven appeared on the top stair with Joe right behind him. "We did," he replied. "I mean, we started to clean it. It's a big job, you know."

"As big as this?" Elizabeth asked.

Steven looked around the attic. "You guys are going to be up here for years!" he exclaimed. "Anyway, Joe and I decided to take a break, so we did some exploring in the area. You'll never guess what we found."

"A severed hand?" Jessica said.

"Better!" Joe said. "A *cave!*"

"With tunnels and bats and everything. The whole bit," Steven added proudly.

"Where?" Jessica asked excitedly. "Show us where it is!"

Steve grinned. "No way! This is *our* cave."

"We're not letting any *girls* in on our discovery," Joe added.

"Then why did you bother to tell us?" Robin demanded.

Steven shrugged. "We just thought you'd want to share in our moment of glory."

"Honestly, Steven," Jessica retorted, "it's not like you discovered *America*. It's just a stupid cave."

Steven frowned. "Come on, Joe. I can see we're not appreciated here."

As the boys climbed down the steep stairs, Jessica grabbed the end of a heavy trunk and began to pull it slowly across the floor. "Could you give me a hand, Robin?"

Robin reached for the other end. "Where are you taking this?" she asked, gasping. "Not far, I hope!"

"Over by the clothes rack."

Stacey helped clear a path for the trunk and then sighed loudly. "I'm thirsty! I could really use a drink."

"Hey, Elizabeth," Jessica called, dropping her end of the trunk. "Why don't you get us something to drink?"

Elizabeth was glancing through Alexandra's diary. "Why should *I* go?"

"*I'll* go, if you want to help move this trunk," Jessica replied.

Elizabeth put down the book and rose to her feet. "No, thanks," she said with a smile. "Want to come, Stacey?"

Stacey looked over at Jessica, who nodded. "Don't work too hard," she told Jessica with a wink.

When they returned a few minutes later, Elizabeth carried a small plastic pitcher of lemonade and Stacey had four paper cups. Jessica was sitting on the floor, panting loudly.

"Amazing!" Elizabeth said. She handed her twin the pitcher of lemonade. "You've actually worked up a sweat!"

"I was moving this, uh, box around," Jessica replied, still breathing hard. "Next time, I'll let you do the heavy work!"

Abruptly, Jessica stood up and stretched. "Come on, you guys. Aren't you starving?"

"*I* am!" Stacey announced.

"Come on, Elizabeth," Jessica cried. "It's time for a lunch break!" She paused as she reached the stairs. "And don't forget that photo album you found."

"I found Alexandra's diary, too," Elizabeth said as she gathered up the album, and the little leather book. "I'm going to put these in the bedroom. I'll meet you guys downstairs."

Elizabeth went to her bedroom and set the album and diary on her bed. She opened the photo album. There before her on the page, looking stern and forbidding in his old-fashioned suit, was the very same man in the portrait on her bedroom wall.

Elizabeth glanced up to compare the photo to

the oil painting. Suddenly a cold shiver ran the length of her spine.

Phineas Whyte had disappeared! In his place was a portrait of a woman in a blue dress, holding a tiny baby in her lap. The painting of Alexandra's father had vanished into thin air!

Five

Elizabeth ran from the room and raced down the stairs. She dashed through the parlor, where four workers in overalls were painting the walls.

She found Jessica and Stacey in the kitchen making peanut-butter sandwiches. "Jess," she began, trying to catch her breath, "would you come upstairs for a minute?"

"Can't it wait? I'm inventing a new sandwich," Jessica said as she searched one of the cupboards. "Peanut butter and maple syrup," she murmured.

Stacey stuck out her tongue. "Gross."

"Please?" Elizabeth pleaded. "I need you to reassure me that I'm not going crazy."

"You're not going crazy," Jessica repeated matter-of-factly. She reached for a can and examined the label. "How about peanut butter and black olives?" she asked Stacey.

"No way!" Stacey said, wrinkling her nose.

"Where's Robin?" Elizabeth pressed. "Maybe she'll go with me."

"She's in the bathroom washing up," Jessica answered. "Peanut butter and tuna fish?"

Elizabeth slumped against the counter and sighed. "There *must* be a logical explanation for this," she murmured.

"There is. Aunt Helen told us we could eat anything we wanted and to be creative."

"That's not what I meant. You'd have to see it to understand."

Jessica glanced at Stacey and rolled her eyes. "Oh, all right, Elizabeth. We'll go, if it'll make you happy. But if we pass out from starvation, it will be your fault."

Elizabeth led Jessica and Stacey upstairs. When they reached her bedroom, she stood in the doorway and pointed toward the wall on which the portrait hung. "There!" she said triumphantly. "Look at that painting and *then* tell me I'm going crazy!"

"You're going crazy," Jessica stated.

"You're going crazy," Stacey repeated.

"But the painting's changed!" Elizabeth cried. "It *was* a man and now it's a—"

"It's *still* a man, as far as I can see," Jessica said dryly.

Elizabeth looked at the painting and saw Phineas Whyte staring back at her. She blinked. "But there was a *different* painting on the wall a few minutes ago!" she insisted.

"I'm sure there's a logical explanation," Jessica assured her twin with a hint of a smile.

Elizabeth dropped onto the edge of the bed and rubbed her eyes. "You're right," she said at last. "I was probably just imagining things."

"Or maybe . . ." Jessica's smile faded and she cast an anxious look at Stacey. "Maybe it's the ghost at work again!"

Stacey glanced around the room nervously. She moved a little closer to Jessica. "But why does he keep bothering us?" she whispered.

"Maybe he doesn't want us to be here. The inn's been empty for almost seventy years, after all," Jessica said.

"Will you please stop talking that way?" Elizabeth asked irritably.

"Well, if it's not a ghost, it seems to me there's only one logical explanation," Jessica replied, turning toward the door.

"What's that?"

"You really *are* going crazy, Lizzie!" Jessica was out of range before the pillow Elizabeth threw could hit her.

Elizabeth got up and slowly followed the other girls into the hallway. The painting *had* changed. She was certain of that. But how, and why, were questions she didn't have any answers for—yet.

Just then Elizabeth noticed the door to one of the empty bedrooms. A brass key sat in the lock. She smiled. *I may have just discovered a way to find the answer*, she thought.

The girls were finishing their lunch when Aunt Helen joined them in the kitchen.

"That garden will be the death of me yet!" she said as she pulled off a pair of soil-covered garden gloves. "Did you girls get enough to eat? Don't forget there's plenty of blueberry pie." She settled into a chair and wiped her brow. "I've still got dozens of geraniums to plant this afternoon," she said, sighing.

"Would you like some help, Aunt Helen?" Elizabeth asked.

"Thank you, Elizabeth." Suddenly Aunt Helen looked worried. "Oh, my! I hope you girls aren't working too hard! This was supposed to be fun, too. You know what they say: all work and no play—"

"Don't worry, Aunt Helen," Robin spoke up. "We *are* having fun. There's lots of weird stuff up in the attic."

"Well, just promise me that tomorrow you'll

do some exploring. Maybe you could visit Holton, do a little shopping."

"Are there many stores in town?" Jessica asked eagerly.

"Let's see now." Aunt Helen began counting on the fingers of her right hand. "There are four, if you count the gas station." She smiled apologetically. "I'm afraid Holton isn't exactly Sweet Valley or San Diego. But I'm sure you'll find something to keep you occupied." She pushed back her chair and stood. "Ready to tackle those geraniums, Elizabeth?"

As she and Elizabeth headed out to the garden, Aunt Helen called over her shoulder, "By the way, the workmen will be painting inside for the next few days, girls. Watch where you put your hands!"

Jessica, Robin, and Stacey returned to the attic, but they quickly grew tired of working. While Jessica and Robin tried on old clothes in front of a cracked mirror, Stacey explored a set of bookshelves filled with interesting odds and ends. As she was reaching up to the highest shelf, she knocked over a can of paint. It landed with a thud, spilling bright red paint all over her right foot. "Oh, no!" she groaned. "What a mess!"

Robin came over to investigate. "Too bad you

didn't spill some white paint. At least it would have matched your sneaker."

Stacey pulled off the sneaker. "I'm going to go rinse it off," she said.

"I'll go with you and get some paper towels to mop this up," Robin said. "We'll be right back, Jessica."

Jessica nodded distractedly as Robin and Stacey headed downstairs. She was trying on a beaded white hat with a long, flowing veil. Jessica twirled around in front of the mirror and admired her image. "I wonder if this was a bridal veil?" she asked aloud.

"It was indeed."

Jessica whirled around to find one of the workers standing behind her.

"Where did you come from?" she asked suspiciously.

"I'm awfully sorry if I startled you, miss," he said, smiling shyly.

Jessica eyed the workman carefully. His eyes were black and his skin was pale, and he was wearing overalls. His jet black hair was parted in the middle and slicked down. It was a very old-fashioned hairstyle, Jessica thought, but on him it seemed appropriate.

"I'm Bill," the workman said, extending his right hand.

"I'm Jessica," she replied, shaking his hand warily.

"You're new to the inn," Bill said, settling himself on a crate. "How do you like it so far?"

"It's OK," Jessica answered. "Of course, it needs a lot of work."

Bill nodded slowly. "It's a grand old house," he said. "I know all about The Lakeview Inn. Ask me anything."

Jessica took off the hat. "How did you know this was a bridal veil?"

Bill smiled and sighed. "Yes," he said, ignoring Jessica's question, "I know things about this place that even your Aunt Helen doesn't know." He reached into a trunk and rummaged through it. At last he pulled out a sheaf of yellowed papers. "These," he said, thumbing through them, "are the plans of The Lakeview Inn. You'll find every nook and cranny of the place marked on these papers. Here." He held one of the pages out to Jessica.

She walked over hesitantly and took the paper from Bill's hand. At first it was just a jumble of lines, but after a few minutes she could see that she was looking at a diagram of the attic.

"Aunt Helen said gold miners used to come here in the 1800s," Jessica said.

Bill nodded. "They did indeed. The parlor

was a saloon back then. The men would come here after a hard day of digging and drink away all their earnings. What they didn't spend on liquor, they lost on poker." He paused and shuffled through the papers. "I'll bet you don't know about the secret passageways," he said slyly.

"Secret what?" Jessica asked incredulously.

"The owners of the inn liked to keep track of the poker games, so they installed secret passageways on the second floor, where the gambling took place every night."

"Where are they?" Jessica asked excitedly.

Bill handed her another sheet of plans and pointed to a long, narrow room between two bedrooms.

"But that's right next to my bedroom!" Jessica exclaimed.

"I told you this place was interesting," Bill said quietly.

Jessica sat down on the floor and traced the lines on the paper with her fingertip. Who would have dreamed that this old, ramshackle house would hold such a wonderful secret?

"Jess? What are you looking at?"

Jessica looked up to see Robin and Stacey at the top of the stairs. "Floor plans of the inn," she explained. "Bill gave them to me."

"Who?" Stacey asked.

Jessica glanced around the attic. "Now, where did he go?" she wondered.

"What are you talking about?" Robin asked.

"Didn't you see a workman just now?"

Stacey and Robin shook their heads.

"That's strange," Jessica murmured. "I guess he had to get back to work."

"Those are plans of the inn?" Stacey asked, peering over Jessica's shoulder.

Jessica pointed to the secret passageway on the paper in front of her. "Just wait until you see this!" she said with a gleam in her eye.

"If I hear one more word about that stupid cave, I'll scream!" Jessica cried that night. She stomped into the bedroom and fell onto her bed.

Elizabeth was arranging a vase of fresh flowers on her nightstand. "I see you've been talking to Steven and Joe," she said.

"They could at least have the decency to tell us where it is," Jessica said, pouting. "Where'd the flowers come from?"

"I found them growing wild in the backyard. I gave most of them to Aunt Helen, and kept these."

Jessica hopped off her bed and walked over to the nightstand. She took a deep whiff of a red rose. "These are beautiful," she murmured. Then she gazed up at the portrait of Phineas

Whyte. "Elizabeth?" she asked thoughtfully, settling next to her sister on the bed. "I've been thinking about the paintings being switched this afternoon. What if it really was caused by something . . . supernatural?"

Elizabeth laughed. "You mean a ghost?"

"Laugh all you want, but do you have a *logical* explanation for what happened?"

"Well, no," she admitted, looking at Jessica suspiciously. "Not yet, anyway. But that doesn't mean I believe in ghosts!"

"And how about Robin and Stacey's room being so cold last night?" Jessica pressed. "How do you explain that?"

"This ghost is a figment of your imagination," Elizabeth answered. She opened the drawer of her nightstand and produced an old-fashioned brass key. "Besides," she said with a smile, "I'm sure he—or she—won't be back tonight."

"What do you mean?" Jessica asked, narrowing her eyes.

"I found this key today. It locks our door from either direction."

"You mean we can lock ourselves in?"

Elizabeth nodded. "I'm going to lock the door and sleep with this key under my pillow all night. That way, only a *real* ghost can get in."

Jessica returned the key to her twin. "Well, I don't see what that's going to accomplish," she declared, crossing her arms over her chest. "It's not going to stop *our* ghost, that's for sure."

"We'll just see about that," Elizabeth replied confidently.

Six

◇

Elizabeth woke the next morning feeling refreshed. She felt under her pillow for the key. It was still there, just where she had put it. She looked at the wall to check the portrait. It was still stern Phineas Whyte, just as it had been the night before.

"Morning, Jess," Elizabeth called.

Jessica rolled over immediately. She was wide awake. "Morning."

"I see my little ghostbusting trick worked after all," Elizabeth said accusingly. "It's funny, isn't it? When I lock the door and no *person* can get in or out, nothing mysterious seems to happen."

Jessica yawned. "It'll take more than one peaceful night to convince me."

Elizabeth kicked off her covers. Suddenly she gasped. "My flowers!" she cried, reaching for the vase on her nightstand. "They're dead!"

Jessica sat up on her elbows. "Cut flowers always wilt," she remarked indifferently.

"But these aren't just wilted," Elizabeth protested. She removed one of the brittle dead roses from the vase. The dry, brown petals crumbled in her hand. "These are so dry, they look like they were in a fire! And there's plenty of water in the vase."

Jessica's eyes widened. "So what's your logical explanation for *this?*" she demanded. "If I were you, I'd apologize to the ghost for not believing, Elizabeth. And I'm getting out of here," she declared. "That is, if you don't mind."

"What?" Elizabeth asked distractedly.

"The key," Jessica prodded. "Would you mind unlocking the door, now that your experiment is over?"

Elizabeth was still examining the dead flowers. "Here—go ahead. I'll be down in a minute."

On her way down to the kitchen for breakfast, Elizabeth paused in the dining room. In the center of the table was a large crystal vase filled with the rest of the flowers she had picked the previous day. But *these* were still fresh and colorful.

The others were already seated at the kitchen table when Elizabeth joined them. "There she is!" Aunt Helen exclaimed, giving Elizabeth a hug. "I wondered what was keeping my star gardener. Did you see how lovely your flowers looked on the dining room table? You can even smell their fragrance in the kitchen."

That's strange, Elizabeth thought. *Why couldn't I smell them when I was in the dining room?*

After breakfast, Aunt Helen told the girls to do some exploring in town. But first Jessica insisted on running upstairs to change her shoes.

"What's the matter with the ones you have on?" Robin asked.

"They don't match my outfit," Jessica replied, tossing her hair over her shoulder. "When I got dressed this morning, I didn't know I'd be going out in *public!* I'll only be a minute."

Jessica ran through the parlor, where she passed several workers. She continued upstairs, changed shoes quickly, and dashed back into the hallway. She was almost at the stairs when Bill stepped out of one of the empty bedrooms.

"Hello, Jessica," he said politely.

"You scared me!" Jessica exclaimed. "What are you doing in there? I thought you guys were working on the parlor."

"I was just looking for a ladder," Bill explained.

Jessica glanced at him suspiciously. She thought it was odd that his overalls were so neat and clean while the workers downstairs wore paint-spattered ones.

"Did you have a chance to check out the secret passageway and the two-way mirror I told you about?" Bill asked.

"Well, I did find the passageway. In my cousins' room, the bookcase opens out, and in mine, the mirror is also a door. But is the mirror also two-way?"

"Yes. The original owner of the inn installed it so he could watch the poker games without being seen."

"How does the mirror work?" Jessica asked curiously. The old inn was getting more interesting by the minute!

"Well, it's like this," Bill said with a sly smile. "When the light is on in your bedroom, and it's dark in the secret passageway, you can see right through the mirror from the passageway into the bedroom. Of course, it works in reverse, too."

"What do you mean?"

"If it's dark in the room and you turn on a light in the secret passageway, then people in the bedroom can see through the mirror into the passageway."

"That's fabulous! We didn't notice it last night because the lights were out in the bedroom. I've got to go now, Bill," she said. "But thanks for the information."

Bill made a formal bow. "My pleasure."

* * *

The girls spent about an hour exploring Holton. At least twenty minutes of that hour was spent at a little drug store on Main Street. While Jessica and Robin bought cosmetics and candy, Elizabeth browsed through the paperback book display.

"Too bad Stacey decided to stay home and help Aunt Helen with the garden," Jessica commented as the girls left the drugstore and began their walk home. "She missed seeing beautiful downtown Holton."

They turned onto the narrow, winding road that led to the inn. The sky had grown overcast and the wind whistled through the tall pines overhead. Elizabeth led the way, while Jessica and Robin straggled behind.

"Slow down, Elizabeth," Jessica complained. "How can I enjoy looking around if you're practically running?"

"I'm walking at a normal speed," Elizabeth insisted. "Besides, when did you get so interested in the scenery? I don't see any boys and I don't see any boutiques. In fact, there's nothing but nature all around us. Now, if there were a mirror . . ."

"Very funny, Elizabeth," Jessica retorted. "It just so happens I *enjoy* nature." She pointed to a small, scruffy stand of trees. "Aren't those interesting-looking trees, Robin?"

"What? Um, yes," Robin agreed. "Very interesting."

"And look at all these rocks!" Jessica said enthusiastically.

"Great rocks!" Robin said.

Elizabeth looked dubiously at her twin and her cousin.

"I wonder if these rocks have gold in them?" Jessica asked, and suddenly stopped.

Elizabeth saw her sister kneel down and stare at the ground. "What is it?"

"Tracks!" Jessica exclaimed, pointing at the ground.

"So?" Elizabeth asked.

"They're sneaker tracks heading away from the road and toward that big pile of boulders." Jessica followed the trail by pointing her finger.

"Yes, so they're sneaker tracks. So what?" Elizabeth asked.

"Don't you get it?" Jessica said. "I'll bet Steven and Joe's cave is right around here! These are their footprints."

Elizabeth knelt down to look at the tracks. "One set looks awfully small."

"Um . . . well, maybe Joe has small feet," Robin suggested.

"We certainly know *Steven's* feet aren't small," Elizabeth said, laughing.

"Let's follow the trail and see if we're right," Jessica suggested.

Elizabeth shrugged. "All right."

Robin nodded in agreement. "I don't like those guys having secrets."

The girls headed off the road, following the sneaker tracks carefully. The tracks led them to a narrow ravine. Boulders rose up all around them, towering over their heads and cutting them off from sight of the road.

"This way!" Jessica called as she followed the sneaker prints until they stopped at the base of a steep hill. There the girls saw a dark, square entrance cut into the hillside.

"That's not a cave," Elizabeth remarked. "It's an old mine shaft."

"You mean to a *gold* mine?" Robin asked excitedly.

"Probably," Elizabeth said as she peered inside. "You see the way those boards have been used to strengthen the walls and hold up the roof? I'll bet this mine is very, very old."

"You don't think the boys found some gold and aren't telling us, do you?" Robin asked.

"Steven keep a secret like that?" Elizabeth said skeptically. "Believe me, if Steven had found gold, we would have heard about it. Besides, this mine has been abandoned for years."

"Do you think Steven and Joe are in there?" Jessica asked, squinting into the darkness.

"Maybe," Elizabeth said. "But without a light we can't go in to look for them."

"Well, it just so happens I have a small flashlight in my purse," Robin said brightly.

"It 'just so happens'?" Elizabeth repeated suspiciously.

"I carry it in case of emergencies like . . . like if the lights go out."

"Even with a light, I don't think we should go in there," Elizabeth cautioned. "The mine shaft could cave in if we stumbled against one of the supports."

"That's true, Elizabeth," Jessica said quickly. "But what if Steven and Joe are in there right now? They may not realize the danger! We have to warn them!"

Elizabeth nodded thoughtfully. "I guess you're right. Get out your flashlight, Robin, and let's all be careful not to touch the walls."

Robin rummaged in her purse and pulled out a very small flashlight. Slowly and very cautiously, the girls stepped into the black mouth of the mine shaft. Immediately the air became cold and damp. Elizabeth's foot struck something that made a clattering sound. All three girls jumped.

Robin shone the light across the uneven floor. "Look," she said. "It's an old hammer."

"It must have been left here by a miner," Elizabeth said. "*Steven!*" she yelled. "Are you in here?"

The sound of her voice was instantly swallowed up. Reluctantly, Elizabeth stepped forward. She glanced over her shoulder to find that the entranceway was a small square of light, very far away.

"I don't think we should go much further," Elizabeth said nervously.

"Oh, don't be a baby, Elizabeth," Jessica scolded. "What are you afraid of? You don't think there's a bear or something living in here, do you?" Suddenly she froze. "What was that?"

"What?" Robin asked.

"Shh! I thought I heard something!"

"What did you hear?" Elizabeth whispered.

"I don't exactly know," Jessica answered. "It sounded like a voice."

"A voice?" Elizabeth asked. "You mean Steven's or Joe's?"

Jessica shook her head. "No. A man's voice. Very low, and I think it was saying, 'get out'!"

"Oh, Jessica," Elizabeth groaned. "Stop trying to—"

Suddenly a bloodcurdling scream echoed down the narrow corridor of the mine shaft.

All three girls screamed in response. Elizabeth tried to move, but she was frozen for that moment.

Then she saw it—a huge, billowing white figure flying toward them! It was speeding from the blackest reaches of the tunnel, screaming as it came!

Seven

◇

"Run!" Jessica bolted toward the entrance to the mine, closely followed by Elizabeth and Robin.

Elizabeth turned to look back at the large white figure, and her foot caught on a rock. She hit the ground with enough force to knock the wind out of her, but she was up on her feet in a second and racing after the other two girls.

As they approached the entrance to the mine shaft Elizabeth paused for just a second and looked back over her shoulder. The ghost, if that was what it was, was no longer in sight.

Quickly Elizabeth reached into her pocket and took out the small notebook she often carried with her. She threw it on the sandy ground in front of the cave and hurried to catch up with Jessica and Robin.

"Wha . . . what do you think that was?" Jessica stammered when they had reached the main road.

"It . . . it looked like . . . a ghost!" Robin squealed.

"It must have been a ghost!" Jessica said. "What else could it have been?"

"Do you think it's the same ghost that's haunting the inn?" Robin asked Elizabeth.

"I don't know *what* it was!" Elizabeth replied. "It certainly *looked* like a ghost."

"It *had* to be a ghost!" Robin added.

"I guess you're right," Elizabeth replied. Suddenly she patted her pocket. "Hey! I lost my notebook!"

"In the mine shaft?" Jessica asked.

"No. It must have been just outside the mine shaft. I heard something fall to the ground, but I was too scared to pay any attention," Elizabeth answered.

"Well, you're not going back after it, are you?" Jessica warned.

"I have to," Elizabeth said firmly.

"You can't! What about the ghost?" Robin asked.

"He didn't chase us out into the sunlight. I'm sure he's stuck in that dark mine shaft. You know how ghosts are." Elizabeth smiled reassuringly. "But just in case, I want you two to stay here at a safe distance. If I get into any trouble, I'll yell and you can go get help."

"We'd better go with you," Jessica said doubtfully.

"No! Absolutely not! I wouldn't want the ghost to get all three of us just because I was clumsy enough to drop my notebook."

Jessica and Robin exchanged a worried look. "Well, all right," Jessica said finally. "But be quick, and be careful!"

"I will," Elizabeth promised. She started off quickly toward the mine shaft. When she reached the pile of boulders that hid the dark entrance from sight of the other two girls, she heard Jessica crying, "Be careful going *back* to the mine, Elizabeth!"

"We wouldn't want you to see the ghost again!" Robin called loudly.

Elizabeth smiled. She picked up her notebook and shoved it back into her pocket. Then she uprooted a tall clump of weeds that was growing by the rocks. Using the weeds as a broom, she carefully smoothed away all the footprints in the sand around the mine shaft's entrance.

Satisfied with her work, Elizabeth threw the weeds aside and ran swiftly back to join her sister and cousin.

"Did you see anything?" Jessica demanded anxiously.

"Not a thing," Elizabeth assured her.

"Well, all I can say is, you're awfully lucky the ghost didn't get you," Robin remarked. "It certainly scared me!"

"Me, too!" Jessica agreed. "How about you, Elizabeth? Weren't you scared?"

Elizabeth paused to consider for a moment before answering. "I was startled," she said at last.

"Just startled?" Jessica protested. "I was *terrified!*"

"And I was terrified, too!" Robin said. "Elizabeth, you act as if being attacked by a ghost is the sort of thing that happens every day."

"Really!" Jessica gave Elizabeth a sidelong look. "Don't you think it was a real ghost?"

Elizabeth shrugged. "It was a real *something*."

"What else could it have been besides a ghost?"

"I don't know," Elizabeth admitted. "But just because you don't understand something doesn't mean you should start believing in the supernatural."

They turned a bend in the road and the inn came into view. "Maybe," Elizabeth said with a small grin, "that ghost was really *Steven*."

"Steven?" Jessica asked.

"It all fits. The ghost was taller than us. Joe is about the same height as we are, but Steven is taller. Tall enough to play the ghost if he put a sheet over his head.''

"How can we find out if it was Steven?" Robin asked innocently.

"Oh, that's easy," Elizabeth said smugly. "This road is the quickest way from the cave to the inn. If it *was* Steven, he couldn't have made it back here before us without passing us on the road. So, logically, if Steven is at the inn, then Steven was not the ghost.''

"And if Steven *is* here at the inn—" Jessica began.

"I'll bet anything we won't find him here," Elizabeth concluded confidently.

The girls opened the front door of the inn and stepped inside. "Aunt Helen!" Elizabeth called out. "We're back!"

"In the billiard room!" Aunt Helen responded.

The girls headed toward the billiard room, which was across from the main parlor. "Is Steven down at the boathouse?" Elizabeth called, casting an I-told-you-so look at her twin.

"No, he isn't," Aunt Helen called back as the girls reached the billiard room. "He's in here with me."

Elizabeth stopped dead in her tracks. Steven was leaning over the pool table with a cue in his hand.

"Steven's been teaching me to play pool," Aunt Helen explained. "He's been trying to teach me the bank shot for the last hour, but I'm afraid I'm a hopeless case."

Jessica quickly reached for Elizabeth's hand. "We're going to get a snack, Aunt Helen."

"We can't tell Aunt Helen about this!" Jessica hissed when they reached the hallway. "She would either think we were crazy, or get worried—and the last thing we want to do is upset her!"

"I was sure it was Steven," Elizabeth mumbled. "It *had* to be Steven!"

"It was a ghost, Elizabeth!" Robin said in exasperation. "Why can't you just accept it?"

"Because," was all that Elizabeth could say.

"There aren't always explanations for everything," Jessica replied. "I've been trying to tell you that."

Elizabeth nodded slowly. "Yes. Maybe . . . maybe you're right, Jessica. Maybe you've been right all along."

After their snack, the girls were in no mood to go back to work in the attic. They spent the afternoon playing pool and eating the brownies Aunt Helen had baked for them. When they finished the first batch they made a second batch themselves.

"I promise we'll work extra hard tomorrow," Elizabeth told Aunt Helen.

Aunt Helen laughed as she helped Jessica pull a tray of brownies out of the oven. "Don't be silly, dear!" she said. "This is your summer vacation, after all."

"But we want to help out," Robin insisted. "It's just that—well, we had sort of a rough morning."

"Is anything wrong, girls?" Aunt Helen asked. "Something I can help you with?"

"Robin just means we wore ourselves out walking," Elizabeth explained quickly.

Aunt Helen nodded. "It's quite a long trek to Holton," she said. "But there are certainly some interesting sights along the way."

"You can say that again!" Elizabeth agreed with a grim smile.

The girls decided to go to bed early that night so they could get a fresh start the next morning.

"Well, I'm ready to go right to sleep," Jessica informed her twin.

"Me, too," Elizabeth said. "But I think I might read Alexandra's diary for a few minutes."

"You're not afraid of turning out the lights, are you?" Jessica teased. "That wouldn't be very *logical*, would it?"

"That's not it at all," Elizabeth said defensively. "I just wanted to read some more of Alexandra Whyte's diary."

"Sure," Jessica said sarcastically. "And I guess you're not at all worried that the ghost of The Lakeview Inn may strike again?"

Elizabeth climbed into her bed and pulled the covers up to her chin. "I don't know exactly how I feel, Jessica. But I do know that I'm too old to sleep with the light on!" She reached over and flipped off her bedside lamp. "Good night."

"What about the diary?"

"I've got some thinking to do instead," Elizabeth answered.

"Well, good night, then." Jessica switched off her own light. "I just hope the ghost can tell us apart. I'm not the one who thinks he's a fake!"

Much later that night Elizabeth woke with a start, certain that she had heard a loud noise of some kind. "Jess?" she whispered.

"Yes, I heard it, too!" came the reply. Elizabeth squinted in the almost total darkness. She could barely make out her sister's silhouette.

"Turn on the light!" Elizabeth urged.

"I tried!" Jessica said grimly. "Both lamps are out!"

After a moment, Elizabeth began to see more clearly. Jessica's outline was distinct, and now the posts of the beds and the big armoire were beginning to appear.

"Where's that light coming from?" Elizabeth whispered.

Jessica gulped. "I . . . I think it's coming from . . . from the mirror on the wall!"

"But that's impossible!" Elizabeth cried.

Slowly the girls climbed out of bed, and together made their way toward the dim, eerie light. Elizabeth could feel her heart pounding frantically. She reached out with trembling fingers to take Jessica's hand, and was relieved to feel that it was steady and calm.

There was now no doubt that a soft, strange light was coming from the mirror itself. The two girls stood side by side, staring at it apprehensively. With a sudden jolt of understanding, Elizabeth realized there was no reflection in the mirror!

Instead, the mirror had somehow turned into a window. Suddenly the light from the mirror became brighter, and as it did Elizabeth began to make out words written on the mirror.

Elizabeth took an involuntary step backward, but could not tear her fascinated gaze from the words, now horribly distinct and written in red:

> *I am coming for you,*
> *Elizabeth Wakefield!*
> *Though you do not believe,*
> *You cannot escape!*

Eight

◇

Jessica watched Elizabeth out of the corner of her eye. Elizabeth's face was pale. The message seemed to terrify her. Then, suddenly, the message began to fade and in its place a horrible face with two glowing eyes appeared. Jessica could not believe what she was seeing. As suddenly as it had appeared, the face was gone. The room was left in complete darkness.

Jessica made her way to her bedside lamp and reached beneath the shade. With trembling fingers, she screwed the light bulb in tightly, and the light came on.

"The lights!" Elizabeth cried. "The lights are back on. How . . . ?"

"I guess . . . I guess the bulb was loose. I just . . . just screwed it back in." Jessica saw that her sister was looking at her with a mixture of fear and curiosity. "Did you see that thing in the mirror?" Jessica demanded.

Elizabeth nodded slowly. "Yes. I saw the message."

Jessica waved her hand impatiently. "I meant the face! Did you see the face, or am I crazy?"

Elizabeth looked closely at her sister before answering. "Yes, Jess. I saw that, too."

"What could it have been?" Jessica cried.

Elizabeth shrugged uncertainly. "I don't know, Jess," she confessed. "Maybe some trick reflection caused by moonlight coming in through the curtains."

"Give me a break, Elizabeth! Do you *really* think that's what it was?"

Elizabeth walked up to the mirror and gingerly touched its cool, hard surface. In it she saw her own reflection. Then she looked toward the window. The moonlight was casting faint shadows on the lacy curtains. "I don't know, Jess," Elizabeth said finally. "I suppose it was some sort of dream. Maybe . . . maybe this is *still* a dream."

"You mean you think you're asleep and dreaming all this?" Jessica demanded incredulously.

"It could be. All I know is that whatever I *thought* I saw in the mirror isn't there anymore. That's the kind of thing that happens in a dream."

"But *I'm* awake!" Jessica protested.

"Are you absolutely sure?" Elizabeth asked.

"Of course I'm sure." Jessica pinched her own cheek. "I felt that."

"That doesn't prove anything," Elizabeth argued. "If we're awake, and all this is really happening, then why didn't Robin and Stacey come running when they heard that noise? Even with these thick old walls, Robin would certainly have heard that."

"Well, there could be a lot of reasons. . . ." Jessica shrugged and looked away. When she looked back again, Elizabeth was nodding as if she had proved something. "All right, Elizabeth," Jessica said in exasperation. "Have it your way! We're asleep and this is all just a dream! A nightmare, I should say. I guess there's nothing for us to do but go back to sleep!"

"If it's a dream, we're *already* asleep," Elizabeth said reasonably.

"Well, if I'm asleep, I should be in bed. And that's where I'm going." Jessica climbed into her bed and pulled the covers up to her chin. After hesitating for a moment, Elizabeth did the same.

"Aren't you going to turn out your light?" Elizabeth asked.

"No way! Besides, you're asleep and having a dream. What do *you* care?" Jessica rolled over onto her side. *What is it going to take to convince her?* she wondered sourly.

* * *

When Jessica awoke the next morning, she saw that Elizabeth was already dressed.

"Hi," Elizabeth said cheerfully. "Sleep well?"

Jessica peered at her sister suspiciously. "How did *you* sleep?"

"Fine," Elizabeth said brightly.

"No . . . nightmares?"

"No. How about you?"

Jessica sat up in bed and rubbed her eyes. Then she reached over and switched off the light by her bed. "No."

"Well, you'd better hurry if you want to get to the bathroom before Robin. She takes almost as much time getting ready as you do." Elizabeth pulled a sweatshirt over her head and headed downstairs to breakfast.

Jessica got to the bathroom at the same time as Robin. Jessica grabbed her cousin's arm, pulled her in, and closed the door.

Robin began to giggle. "We heard you guys get up last night!" she said. "I guess the plan worked! Is Elizabeth ready to admit that ghosts are real?"

"Not exactly," Jessica grumbled.

"What do you mean, 'not exactly'? Didn't she see the message? I thought it was great: 'I am coming for you, Elizabeth Wakefield! Though you do not believe, you cannot escape!' "

"She saw it just fine. But then she came up with the idea that it was all a dream!" Jessica threw up her hands in frustration. "Who could have guessed she'd come up with some theory like that?"

"How could she think it was a dream?"

"She said that if we were awake and it was real, you and Stacey would have heard the noise and come to see what was wrong."

Robin sagged against the wall. "I guess we should have thought of that. But we had to set up the message and—"

"And show that creepy mask," Jessica interrupted. "By the way, when did you find that? It even scared *me*!"

"What mask?" Robin asked blankly.

"The face. The mask with the glowing eyes." Jessica shivered. "It was truly gross!"

"What are you talking about?" Robin asked.

"Don't try to trick me, Robin," Jessica said. "I'm the one who planned this whole ghost thing. You know perfectly well which mask I'm talking about."

"Now *you're* trying to trick *me*," Robin said. "All we did was write the note with the red lipstick we bought at the drugstore."

"Then what was that awful face?" Jessica wondered.

Robin laughed. "Good try, Jessica, but if you can't manage to scare Elizabeth, don't think you can scare me!"

After breakfast, Jessica, Robin, and Stacey jumped up from the kitchen table and raced for the attic. Elizabeth, Steven, and Joe helped Aunt Helen with the dishes. Then the boys headed for the boathouse, and Elizabeth went up to the attic.

"Hi, guys," Elizabeth said brightly. "Aunt Helen asked me to help her in the garden today, so I guess I won't be able to help you up here."

"How come she asked *you?*" Robin asked.

"You weren't around," Elizabeth said, smiling contentedly. She took a step back down the stairs. "See you later. I'll be thinking of you while I'm out in the beautiful sunlight."

"Don't rub it in," Jessica groaned. "I didn't realize how much work there was to be done up here! If I had, I would have stayed in Sweet Valley!"

Elizabeth climbed down the staircase, stopped by her bedroom to pick up her backpack, then headed outside. She was *not* spending the day in the garden.

She walked quickly on the road toward town. When she reached the turn-off to Steven and Joe's "cave," she checked behind her to make sure she wasn't being watched. Then she hurried to the mine shaft's dark entrance.

There she stopped and looked down at the ground. The sand that she had brushed smooth with the weeds showed two clear sets of footprints.

Just as I thought. Two sets of prints, and both heading out of the cave!

Elizabeth pulled her notebook from her pocket, then opened her backpack and took out a plastic ruler. Kneeling carefully in the sand, she measured the footprints—first one set and then the other—and wrote down the sizes in her notebook.

When she stood up, Elizabeth was smiling broadly. "Now we'll see."

Elizabeth brushed the sand from her knees and quickly made her way back to the inn. Once inside, she climbed the stairs to the second floor, being careful not to let Aunt Helen see her. *First stop—Steven and Joe's room*, she thought.

Carefully, Elizabeth tiptoed into the boys' room and measured one of her brother's shoes, noting the length in her notebook. Then she did the same for one of Joe's shoes.

Now I'm getting warmer, she thought.

She returned the boys' shoes to where she'd found them, then proceeded down the hall to Robin and Stacey's room. In their closet she found a pair of shoes that she knew were too small to belong to Robin. She picked them up and again measured carefully.

Perfect! One mystery solved!

Elizabeth returned Stacey's shoes to the closet and began to tiptoe toward the door. Then something she noticed made her stop.

Next to the closet stood a bookcase that extended from floor to ceiling. What was it about the bookcase that had attracted her attention?

She looked down. That was it! The carpet!

Elizabeth dropped to her knees and examined the carpet in front of the bookcase. The fibers had been brushed back. It looked as if something had been pulled across it, forming a fanlike shape.

"What could possibly . . ." Suddenly Elizabeth snapped her fingers. *The Mystery at the Mansion.* It was one of the first Amanda Howard stories she had ever read. And in the book, there was a clue just like this!

Elizabeth straightened up and began to pull books out of the bookcase. After several minutes she found a tiny button that would release the bookcase, allowing it to open like a door.

Elizabeth pushed the button and pulled on the bookcase. It swung open easily but rubbed on the carpet, leaving the telltale clue.

With the bookcase all the way open, the secret room behind it was in full view. Elizabeth stepped inside the small area and saw a piece of white posterboard on the floor. The words on it were written with what looked like bright red lipstick. " 'I am coming for you, Elizabeth Wakefield!' " she read aloud.

Then Elizabeth noticed she could see through a sort of dark window into her own bedroom. "A two-way mirror," she said, nodding her head in understanding. "Very clever. Robin sat in here with this message and waited till she could see we were in bed. Then she turned on the light here in the secret room and held the message up to the two-way mirror for me to see. But how did Jessica and Robin find out about this room?"

Then Elizabeth pushed against the mirror. Slowly it opened into her own bedroom. "A secret door," she mused. "Amanda Howard herself would be proud of my detective work." Her expression darkened. "And Jessica has been very clever, too. But we'll see who has the last laugh!"

Nine

◇

"Shh! I hear someone coming!" Jessica warned. Robin and Stacey stopped talking and listened to the sound of feet climbing the stairs to the attic.

"It's probably Elizabeth," Robin whispered. "We should act as if we've been working. Stacey, go move that box over there!"

"Hello, everyone," Elizabeth called as she reached the top of the stairs. She flopped into an old rocking chair and stared glumly down at the floor.

"What's the matter, Elizabeth?" Stacey asked.

"Yeah, you look depressed," Robin added.

Elizabeth sighed heavily. "I've been thinking and thinking," she said. "And I just can't figure it out."

"What can't you figure out, Elizabeth?" Jessica asked hopefully.

"What happened last night," Elizabeth explained. "I just can't explain it. I . . . I thought it was all a dream."

"Aha!" Jessica cried. "So you're willing to admit it *was* real! I *told* you it wasn't a dream!" She looked carefully at her twin. "So why did you pretend this morning that nothing had happened?"

"I guess because I just wanted it all to go away. I wanted to believe it really *was* just a nightmare." Elizabeth leaned forward and rested her head on her hands. "But I thought about it over and over, and I've finally decided it had to be real."

"The message in the mirror?"

"Uh-huh."

"And you also admit the awful face with the glowing eyes was real?" Jessica continued, ignoring Robin's suspicious glance.

"That, too," Elizabeth agreed sadly. "I can't believe I've been so wrong," she went on. "I've always believed that everything has a logical explanation. Now—well, I'm just not sure anymore."

"*Not sure!*" Jessica cried. "Do you mean you're still not sure it was a ghost?"

Elizabeth looked away thoughtfully. "I'm not sure what it was. But I'm willing to consider that it *might* have been a ghost."

Jessica rolled her eyes. She'd never realized how stubborn her twin could be.

"Well, I'm going back down to help Aunt Helen make lunch. I'll call when it's ready," Elizabeth said as she got to her feet.

After she was gone, Jessica shook her head in frustration. "I guess we're going to have to come up with at least one more trick to convince her."

Robin sighed. "Well, I'm all out of ideas."

"We'll think of something," Jessica declared confidently. "I'm not going to quit until Elizabeth finally admits that not everything in the world can be explained logically. She may be stubborn, but so am I!"

"Girls, would you be willing to take a break from your attic cleaning the day after tomorrow?" Aunt Helen asked during lunch.

"Are you kidding?" Jessica exclaimed. "We'd *love* it!" When Elizabeth shot her a warning look, Jessica quickly added, "Not that we aren't having fun working in the attic, of course!"

Aunt Helen laughed merrily. "I realize being stuck up there is not the most exciting way to spend your summer vacation, girls. Gold Rush Day will be a chance for you to have some fun."

"Gold Rush Day?" Robin repeated. "What's that?"

"It's an annual celebration in Holton," Aunt Helen explained. "Every summer local residents and visitors dress up in old-time costumes. The town sponsors games, and townspeople provide food and crafts for sale. I've never been to Gold Rush Day before, but from what I've read in the paper, it's quite a big event."

"It sounds like lots of fun!" Elizabeth said enthusiastically.

"It'll be fun for me, too," Aunt Helen said. "I'm hoping to see some of the people I knew when I visited as a youngster."

"And there'll be stuff to *buy!*" Jessica added excitedly.

After lunch the girls were anxious to return to the attic to search for costumes. Everyone, that is, except Elizabeth.

Elizabeth dashed out the front door. Several workers were repairing the sagging front porch, and she waved to them as she passed by. Elizabeth found Steven and Joe in the boathouse trying to straighten out a tangled coil of thick, bristly rope. "Hi, boys," she called out.

"Hey!" Steven yelled. "No girls allowed. This is a job for *men!*"

"Yeah," Joe added. "Isn't there some dusting you can do back at the inn?"

"I suppose there is," Elizabeth answered sweetly. "But I find *measuring* much more interesting."

"Measuring?" Joe asked.

"Yes. Measuring footprints."

Steven dropped the rope and looked at his sister. "What are you talking about?"

"I'm talking about the two sets of footprints leading out of your secret 'cave,' Steven." Elizabeth crossed her arms over her chest and smiled. "Yesterday, after we found the mine shaft and the—" she cleared her throat, "*ghost* scared us off, I smoothed out the ground near the entrance. Today I went back and found two sets of footprints. Both were coming *out* of the mine shaft, which means whoever made them had to have already been *inside* when I was there."

Joe's eyes darted nervously in Steven's direction.

"We weren't anywhere near the cave yesterday," Steven blurted. "You saw us at the inn, playing pool with Aunt Helen!"

Elizabeth shook her head. "No, Steven. I saw *you*. I didn't see Joe. I admit I was fooled at first, because the 'ghost' was too tall to be Joe. But then I realized that the other set of footprints belonged to Stacey."

"So what?" Steven said gruffly. "You've been reading too many of those mysteries. Now get lost, squirt. We're trying to work."

Elizabeth could see the guilty look in his eyes. "So I figured out how you did it," Elizabeth continued. "Steven, you stayed at the inn so that

Aunt Helen could give you an alibi, while Joe and Stacey went down to the cave. The 'ghost' was so tall because it was really Stacey sitting on Joe's shoulders."

Steven and Joe looked at each other sheepishly.

"There goes all our fun," Steven said unhappily.

"Not necessarily," Elizabeth responded, a gleam in her eye.

"What do you mean?" Steven asked. "You're on to us now. We could never trick you again."

"That's true," Elizabeth agreed. "But what if you switched sides in the spook war? I know you were helping Jessica to scare me. Now you could help me—"

"To scare Jessica!" Steven finished her sentence.

"Exactly. She has it coming."

"What do you have in mind?" Steven asked, grinning wickedly.

Elizabeth looked around the jumbled boathouse. Then she pointed at a small wooden raft only a few feet long. "There. That's what I need."

"The float? What for?" Joe asked.

"If you can find a couple of sticks, a hammer, some nails, and a rope, I'll show you." Elizabeth rolled up her sleeves.

Half an hour later, they had finished. A six-foot-long board was sticking straight up from the wooden float, just like the mast of a sailboat. Another stick was nailed across the "mast" to form a cross-shaped hanger. And on the hanger they had wrapped an old white sail.

Steven stood back and looked at their creation. "I still don't get it."

"It's easy," Elizabeth explained. "Tonight, just after dinner, Joe will take the rowboat and row across to the other side of the inlet. As he rows, he'll be pulling one end of this big rope across with him."

"I *still* don't get it," Steven confessed.

"The other end of the rope will be attached to this float. Then, we wait until bedtime. Jessica didn't get much sleep last night, so she'll be ready to go to bed early. At least, I hope she will. Meanwhile, you guys will be on the other side of the inlet. We'll arrange some kind of signal and I'll get Jessica to stand in front of the window."

"OK. Then what?" Joe asked, rubbing his hands together.

"Then, as she's looking out at the water, Joe will start to pull on the rope, and the float will begin to glide across the water."

Suddenly Steven laughed. "I get it! The float glides across the water, and the sail will flap in the breeze. From a distance it will look as if some ghostly white figure is floating across the water! Great plan! Jessica will *never* figure it out!"

Joe shook his head ruefully. "I hate to admit it, but that's as sneaky as something *I* would think of!"

"Yes. It *is* a very clever plan."

All three of them spun around at the sound of the strange voice. In the doorway stood a young man wearing a pair of overalls.

"I hope I didn't startle you," the man said. "My name is Bill."

"We didn't hear you come in," Steven said. "Who are you?"

"I'm one of the workers," Bill replied. "I knocked, but you were too busy discussing your plan to notice. I don't mean to be rude, but I couldn't help overhearing your little conspiracy."

Steven sighed. "Are you going to tell our Aunt Helen?"

Bill laughed. "No. No, indeed! I think it's a very clever plan. I was going to suggest an improvement."

"An improvement?" Elizabeth echoed.

"Yes. You see, the moon won't come out tonight until very late, so your 'ghost' will be nearly invisible from the inn. It's very dark out on the water at night."

"I hadn't thought about that," Elizabeth admitted.

"It's easily remedied," Bill said reassuringly. "Simply place a light on the raft with the beam shining upward onto the sail. That way your 'ghost' will seem to glow, and it will be easily seen from any window in the inn."

"Great idea!" Joe said enthusiastically.

"There's a flashlight over there in the tool box," Bill added.

Once Steven found the light, he fixed it in place on the raft. After a few minutes' work, the group was satisfied.

"Thanks for the suggestion, Bill," Elizabeth said. But when she turned around, he was gone.

"I'm just *exhausted*," Elizabeth said as she and the other girls sat in the living room after dinner.

"Where are Steven and Joe?" Robin asked.

"They're around somewhere," Elizabeth assured her.

"Why are you suddenly interested in them?" Jessica wondered.

"Robin *likes* Joe," Stacey teased.

"I do not!" Robin said hotly. "Take that back!"

"Aren't you guys tired?" Elizabeth asked.

"Of course I'm tired," Jessica replied. "I was up half the night being bothered by a you-know-what! A you-know-what you still don't believe in!"

"I have an idea," Elizabeth said suddenly. "Let's all go up to my room and see if we can come up with an explanation for what happened last night."

When they reached the twins' bedroom, Jessica walked over to the mirror and pointed. "It was right there. The message warning Elizabeth *and*"—she looked pointedly at Robin—"the ghost's face!"

Elizabeth walked over to the window. "I still wonder if it could have been some trick of the moonlight coming in through the curtains." She reached up and pulled the curtains closed. Then she opened them again and glanced back at the mirror.

There's the signal, boys, she thought to herself. *Now it's up to you!*

Elizabeth gazed out the window as if she were still lost in thought. Suddenly she stiffened.

"Come . . . come here! L-look!" Elizabeth cried. She raised her hand and pointed out the window. Her face wore an expression of horror.

Jessica rushed to the window, followed closely by Robin and Stacey. The girls stared as a white figure, glowing with an eerie light, glided across the black water.

Elizabeth glanced at her sister and was pleased to see the color draining from Jessica's face.

"It's . . . it's—" Robin began.

"A ghost!" Jessica finished.

"A *real* ghost!" Stacey wailed.

"It *is* a ghost!" Elizabeth joined in. "Now I believe! I'm finally, really convinced!"

"But it . . ." Jessica mumbled.

"Yes?" Elizabeth asked. "You were going to say—"

Suddenly an explosion like fireworks lit up the sky. The "ghost" burst into bright, blinding flames and then roared upward like a rocket into the night!

For a moment the entire area was bathed in an eerie white glow. Then, just as suddenly as it had appeared, the light vanished, and the night closed in around The Lakeview Inn.

Ten

The girls jumped back from the window. Jessica was wide-eyed, and Stacey began to sniffle. Robin put her arm around her little sister.

What was that? Elizabeth wondered. *We hadn't planned that!*

Robin led Stacey over to one of the beds and sat down beside her. "Don't worry, Stace," Robin reassured her. "Whatever it was, it's way out on the water and won't get us in here."

"But what *was* it?" Stacey asked.

"I don't know." Robin looked at Jessica questioningly. Elizabeth saw Jessica shake her head slightly.

"I guess it was a ghost," Elizabeth said brightly. "You guys have been trying to convince me for days that there's a real ghost at The Lakeview Inn, and now I'm convinced."

"But, Elizabeth—" Stacey began.

Jessica glared at her younger cousin and Stacey fell silent.

"What were you going to say, Stacey?" Elizabeth prompted.

"Um, nothing," Stacey said finally.

All right, you three, Elizabeth thought, *if that's the way you want to be, fine. I guess you still haven't learned your lesson.* Elizabeth forced herself to yawn loudly. "You know, I'm still sleepy. I guess all this excitement kind of wore me out."

"*Sleepy!*" Jessica echoed incredulously. "How can you possibly be sleepy after you just watched a ghost walk across the lake and explode?"

"I think it's fascinating that ghosts really do exist," Elizabeth said, "but I'm certainly not going to let that keep me up all night."

"You're not scared?" Robin asked.

"Scared?" Elizabeth repeated thoughtfully. "Not scared, exactly. Just interested. I'd like to learn more about our friend the ghost."

"You're nuts!" Robin said, jumping off the bed. "It's *you* the ghost is after!"

"Do you think so?" Elizabeth wondered calmly. "I think he's after *all* of us."

Jessica and Robin exchanged a meaningful look.

Elizabeth smiled again as she walked toward the bedroom door and opened it. "I'm going to the bathroom to get ready for bed. Robin, if you and Stacey are too frightened to go back to your room, I'd be glad to walk you there. I could even tuck you in."

Elizabeth stepped into the hallway and closed the door behind her. She could barely keep herself from laughing as she heard the muffled voices of the other three girls.

"If this is some trick of yours, Jessica—" Robin began.

"Trick of *mine?*" Jessica said hotly. "You were the one who started with that stupid mask in the mirror!"

Feeling quite pleased with herself, Elizabeth walked along the hallway to Steven and Joe's room. She knocked softly, then stepped inside quickly.

Steven and Joe were just taking off their muddy shoes. "Great job, you guys!" Elizabeth said enthusiastically.

The two boys looked at her with guarded expressions and said nothing.

"It was perfect!" Elizabeth continued. "It looked *exactly* like a ghost walking across the water. And that explosion! I don't know *how* you did it, but it was great. It even scared *me!*"

Again, the two boys looked at each other uncertainly.

A shiver slowly crawled up the back of Elizabeth's neck. "How . . . how *did* you make it explode?" she asked softly.

Steven shook his head slowly. "We didn't."

"We did just what we planned. It exploded all on its own," Joe added.

"Sure," Elizabeth said doubtfully.

"No. We mean it," Steven said grimly. "It just blew up! I swear it, Elizabeth. It just happened."

Elizabeth frowned. "But how could it just happen?"

Joe shrugged. "We can't figure it out."

"The only thing we can think of is that somehow the flashlight caused a spark," Steven said.

"Maybe there was something flammable on the sailcloth," Elizabeth suggested. "Then if there *was* a spark, it could . . ."

Steven nodded doubtfully. "I guess it's possible. It doesn't make much sense, but I guess it *could* have happened that way."

"Yeah." Joe seemed glad to accept any kind of explanation. "That must be it."

"So were Jess and Robin scared?" Steven asked.

Elizabeth laughed. "Very scared. Not quite scared enough to confess everything they've been up to, though. So we're going to have to go ahead with plan number two."

The boys grinned. "Just let us know when the time is right," Joe said enthusiastically.

"We'll be ready," Steven declared. "I just hope there are no surprises with the next trick!"

"I feel as if I've been in this attic for months," Jessica moaned the next day.

"Well, if you would *work* instead of *complaining* all the time, we'd be done by now!" Elizabeth snapped.

All four girls were sleepy. Robin and Stacey had spent the night in Jessica and Elizabeth's room. Elizabeth had shared her bed with Jessica, who jumped every time the house creaked or a cricket chirped.

"I'm going to fall asleep standing up," Robin said as she picked through a box of dusty old records.

"I think I *am* asleep," Stacey added, slumping down onto a wooden crate.

"Robin, why don't you and Stacey take a nap?" Elizabeth suggested. "Jessica and I will keep working."

"Thanks a *lot*," Jessica said.

"Then, when Robin and Stacey come back, it will be our turn to take a nap," Elizabeth explained.

"That sounds good to me. Come on, Stace,"

Robin said with a yawn. "Just an hour of sleep and we'll trade with you guys."

"Don't worry," Jessica called. "If you take longer than an hour, I'll personally come and wake you up!"

Robin and Stacey trudged down the stairs and Jessica glared at her sister. "How come *we* have to stay here and work?"

"Because we haven't accomplished anything yet," Elizabeth said.

"How can we do all this work when we're being haunted by a bloodthirsty ghost?" Jessica whined.

Elizabeth looked at her sister slyly. "You know, Jess, you didn't seem very worried about the ghost until yesterday, when we saw it on the lake."

Jessica avoided her twin's eyes. "Um . . . that's because . . ."

"Uh-huh," Elizabeth responded dryly.

With a sudden burst of energy, Jessica reached for a pile of linens. "Let's stop talking about ghosts and get to work!"

After fifteen minutes of sorting through the gigantic pile of old sheets and comforters, Jessica could barely keep her eyes open.

Jessica searched the attic for her sister. Elizabeth was out of sight behind a pile of boxes filled with books. *She won't even notice if I just lie down here for a minute and rest my eyes*, Jessica thought. The pile of down comforters looked as soft and inviting as any bed. She lay down and let her eyes close. *Just for one minute, then back to work before Elizabeth notices.*

Jessica pulled a comforter up to her chin. She could hear Elizabeth humming. The tune seemed strangely familiar. Then, as Jessica slipped into sleep, she thought, *Why is Elizabeth humming a lullaby?*

Jessica's eyes snapped open suddenly.

Where am I? she wondered. She couldn't see a thing. It was pitch dark all around her.

Is it nighttime? Am I in bed?

Then she felt the jumbled pile of comforters and sheets beneath her and realized she was definitely *not* in bed.

I'm still in the attic! she remembered, sitting up abruptly. "Lizzie?" she called.

There was no answer. Jessica listened, but all she could hear was the sound of her own heart beating. "Somebody turn on the light!" she called, but still there was no answer.

Then she heard the sound.

"Wha—what was that?" she cried, her heart galloping in her chest.

The sound came again, a loud creaking that seemed to be coming from only a few feet away.

"Is s-s-someone there?" she whimpered.

The creaking came again. Jessica climbed to her feet. "All right," she said bravely, "whoever's there had better quit these stupid games, because I'm not scared!"

But when the creaking sounded even closer, Jessica glanced around in panic. Whatever it was was between her and the stairs. She was trapped!

Then she saw a dim light at the farthest end of the attic. She remembered the tiny window that looked out over the yard. Aunt Helen was probably working in the garden. If she could just get to that window, she would be able to yell for help!

Jessica began inching her way toward the window. But in the dark she caught her foot on a box and fell to the floor with a thud.

Jessica stumbled to her feet and ran desperately in the direction of the window. She looked back over her shoulder but still could not see what was following her.

Jessica reached the window and tore at the latch. The window had not been opened in years. It took all of her strength to pry it open even a few inches.

Then she felt something that made her blood freeze. It was as if someone was standing right at her shoulder.

"I've come for you-u, Jessica-a-a," it whispered.

Slowly, stiff with terror, Jessica turned. The figure floated in midair and was a sickly greenish white.

It was a ghost—a tall, billowy figure topped by a horrible face, its eyes glowing.

Jessica shoved at the window in a final, desperate effort to open it. The second it opened, Jessica stuck out her head and screamed with all her might.

Eleven

Elizabeth was heading out to the garden to pick some wild raspberries for Aunt Helen when she heard the scream.

At first she couldn't tell where it was coming from. Then she looked up and saw the open attic window.

Jessica was hanging halfway out and looked as if she was going to jump at any moment!

"*No!*" Elizabeth cried. "Jess, stay there! I'm coming!" Sick with fear, Elizabeth tore back into the inn.

By the time she reached the top of the staircase that led into the attic, she was panting heavily. The attic was as black as night, except for the tiny rectangle of light from the window Jessica was leaning out of.

"I'm coming, Jess!" Elizabeth cried again. She

clawed at the air overhead, trying to catch the light chain. *Where is it?* she thought desperately.

Suddenly the light came on. Elizabeth didn't stop to wonder how it had happened. In the blink of an eye she was at her sister's side, easing her back inside.

"It was after me!" Jessica cried. "It was right there!"

Elizabeth pulled her sister into a standing position and put her arms around her. "I'm sorry, Jess. I'm so sorry. This has gone far enough! You were almost hurt!"

"It was right there!" Jessica repeated. "It—it—"

"Calm down now, Jessica. It's OK." Elizabeth led her twin toward the staircase. "That does it. We're going to put an end to all this right now!" Elizabeth vowed.

Elizabeth sat Jessica down on her bed and made her promise not to move. Then she went into the next bedroom and woke Robin and Stacey.

"What's going on?" Robin asked grumpily, rubbing the sleep from her eyes. "Is it already time for us to get up?"

"It's time for all of us to come clean," Elizabeth said. "You two go to our room and wait there with Jessica. I have to bring some raspberries to

Aunt Helen or she'll wonder what happened to me. I can't believe she didn't hear Jessica scream!"

By the time Elizabeth returned to her room, Robin and Stacey had joined Jessica. The three fell silent as soon as she entered.

Elizabeth sighed. "The first thing I have to tell you all is that you can stop whispering behind my back. I know all about your little conspiracy."

"What do you mean?" Robin asked weakly.

"I mean that I know you and Jessica and Stacey have been trying to convince me that there's a ghost at The Lakeview Inn." Elizabeth stood with her hands on her hips. "All this started because Jessica wanted to convince me that not everything in the world is logical."

"The ghost that almost chased me out of the attic window wasn't logical, Elizabeth!" Jessica argued.

"You're wrong, Jess," Elizabeth said quietly. "I was responsible for that."

"You!" Jessica exploded.

"Yes. I'm sorry it went too far, but *you* started it!"

Jessica looked away evasively. "I still don't know what you're talking about."

"Then I'll explain it all . . . very *logically*," Elizabeth responded. "Let's start at the beginning. First, there was the cold bedroom on the night we arrived. I suspected Robin and Stacey were faking when they came into our bedroom claiming they were freezing. Then, when we went into their room to see for ourselves, I knew it was a trick."

"But the room *was* cold," Stacey pointed out.

Elizabeth smiled. "Yes, but why was it cold? You were very clever to turn off the radiator and open all the windows."

"The windows were closed and the radiator was on," Jessica said. "I saw you check them."

Elizabeth nodded. "I did check them. But the radiator was making a snapping sound, the sound it makes when it has just begun to warm up. It was obvious that it had been turned off, and then, just before Robin and Stacey came to wake us up, turned back on. The radiator itself was warm to the touch, but it hadn't had time to heat the rest of the room."

"That doesn't prove anything," Robin said.

"But there was also the blue eyeshadow you wore the next day, Robin. The same color blue as your *supposedly* cold lips."

Elizabeth crossed her arms in satisfaction and then continued. "Then came the mysterious changing painting. This was a very clever trick, Jess, but by using logic, I was able to figure it out."

"Oh, please, tell us," Jessica said sarcastically.

"I will," Elizabeth replied. "It was all a matter of timing. We were all together in the attic when

Jessica talked me into going down to the kitchen to get some lemonade. While I was away, Jessica ran downstairs and switched the paintings. When I got back with the lemonade, Jessica, I noticed you were panting, as though you'd been running. Of course, at the time I didn't realize what it meant.

"Later, when I'd noticed the paintings had been switched, I ran to get Jessica and show her. Jessica came along, but very slowly, being sure to give Robin plenty of time to switch the paintings back and make me look like a fool."

Robin tried to hide a smile behind her hand.

"There's no way either Robin or I would be strong enough to carry a painting with such a huge frame," Jessica argued.

"No, you're right," Elizabeth said. "That's when I began to suspect the boys were in on this, too."

Robin looked at Jessica and shook her head. "She knows."

"Shh," Jessica hissed.

"Give up, Jess," Elizabeth said. "I know it *all*."

"Really?" Jessica taunted. "How about the flowers that mysteriously died?"

"They didn't die. They were baked." Elizabeth watched Jessica wince. "I knew you'd baked them in the oven to dry them out because the next morning Aunt Helen remarked on the powerful flower smell in the kitchen."

"But you locked the door and kept the key under your pillow," Jessica pointed out. "How could I possibly have gotten the flowers out in the middle of the night and taken them to the kitchen?"

"Well, I have to admit, Jessica, *that* was your greatest accomplishment. For a while you had me totally baffled. That is, until I found the secret passage," Elizabeth answered.

Jessica, Robin, and Stacey groaned in unison.

"I can't believe you found it. How did you ever do it?" Jessica asked.

"It was the mine shaft that led me to the secret passage," Elizabeth explained. "You remember when we were all scared by the so-called ghost? Well, I told you I had dropped my notebook and had to go back for it. Actually, I had dropped the notebook deliberately so I would have an excuse to go back and wipe away all the footprints."

"But why?" Robin asked.

"Because I expected to find new footprints left by Steven and Joe. I have to confess I was *very* surprised when we got back to the inn and I saw Steven had been here all afternoon. That was very clever of you, Jessica, making sure he had an alibi. You knew he'd be the first person I'd suspect."

"Thanks, but I guess it wasn't clever enough," Jessica said glumly.

"No, not quite," Elizabeth agreed. "The next day I sneaked back to the mine shaft and found two sets of footprints leading out of it. I measured them and compared the measurements to Joe's and Stacey's shoes. They matched perfectly."

"You still haven't explained how you found the secret passage," Stacey said.

"That was my finest piece of detective work," Elizabeth said proudly. "The carpet in your bedroom extends right to the bottom of the secret bookcase. When it's swung open, it leaves a fan-shaped mark. Of course," she said loftily, "most people would never have noticed it. But I saw it as a very obvious clue. It only took a few minutes to find the button in the bookcase and to open it."

"I suppose now you think you're the smartest person in the world!" Jessica cried.

"Not the smartest," Elizabeth said with false modesty. "Just very, very logical."

"So then you decided to get your revenge on us, right?" Jessica said. "I don't know how you did it, but I suppose you were responsible for the ghost on the lake?"

"It was my idea," Elizabeth said, grinning. "But I could never have done it without Steven and Joe."

"*Steven and Joe?*" Jessica cried. "But they were on *our* side!"

"Steven and Joe didn't care whose side they were on. They just wanted to have fun," Elizabeth explained.

"Those traitors!" Robin said angrily.

"I told you not to trust boys," Stacey added.

"The only thing I don't understand," Elizabeth continued, "is how you made that awful ghost face in the mirror. There's no way you bought such a realistic mask in Holton! Did you bring it all the way from home?"

"Oh, *that!*" Jessica gave Robin a dirty look. "That was Robin's little trick to scare me, too."

"Jessica, I told you, I don't have any idea what you're talking about," Robin protested.

"Right," Jessica said sarcastically. "It's OK if you want to keep your dumb little secret. Besides, I wasn't really scared."

"You were scared today, though, Jess," Elizabeth said apologetically. "That's why I decided we had to stop this stupid game. I almost scared you into jumping out of the window! I'm really sorry about that. I didn't think the tape recording of creaking footsteps would scare you that much."

"Recording? So *that's* what it was. Well, the

creaking sound scared me, all right. I mean, it was pitch black up there!"

"Why did you turn off the lights?" Elizabeth asked.

"*Me?* I didn't turn off the lights. I woke up and it was totally dark!"

"Then who . . . ?" After a moment Elizabeth snapped her fingers. "It must have been Steven! Count on him to take it too far. He and Joe *must* have been responsible for my lake ghost exploding, even though they denied it."

"Anyway, it wasn't the tape recording that made me want to jump," Jessica said. "It was the ghost! How did you manage *that?*"

Elizabeth looked blankly at her sister. "What ghost? What are you talking about?"

"The tall, floating thing with the glowing eyes. It scared me to death!"

Elizabeth looked at her sister with a mixture of suspicion and confusion. "Are you trying to trick me again?"

"Are you trying to trick *me?*" Jessica retorted. "It looked just like the ghost in the mirror." She turned to Robin. "You?"

"I told you, I don't know what you're talking about!" Robin sprang to her feet in exasperation. "How could I have been dressed up as a ghost and chasing you around the attic? Elizabeth found me down here, asleep!"

"That's true," Elizabeth said quietly.

The four girls all looked at each other uneasily. Then Elizabeth said, "Steven and Joe."

"Of course," Robin agreed with relief. "Steven and Joe. Who else could it have been?"

"Boys!" Stacey said, tossing her hair.

"Well, at least this whole stupid thing is over," Elizabeth said. "Let's go get something to eat. Detective work makes my hungry!"

She led the way out of the room, followed closely by Robin and Stacey. Jessica stayed behind for a moment and looked thoughtfully at the mirror.

Over? she wondered. *Maybe not, Elizabeth.* She took a deep, shaky breath. Steven and Joe couldn't have been responsible for the ghost in the mirror. *They had never known about the secret passage!*

Twelve

"Have you decided what you're going to wear to Gold Rush Day?" Aunt Helen asked Elizabeth the next morning.

Elizabeth and Stacey were sitting on the porch swing looking at the photo album Elizabeth had discovered in the attic. "Stacey suggested we look through this album for some ideas of what to wear," Elizabeth replied. "But these photos are from the wrong era."

Aunt Helen settled into a wicker rocking chair. "I heard Jessica and Robin heading for the attic," she said. "There may be some old clothes up there that belonged to Alexandra's family." She glanced around her with a satisfied smile. "The workmen did a wonderful job repairing the porch, don't you think?"

Elizabeth didn't answer. She was staring intently at a page of yellowed photos. Something about them made her feel vaguely uneasy.

"Elizabeth?" Aunt Helen asked. "Is something wrong?"

"I'm sorry, Aunt Helen," Elizabeth said distractedly. "What did you say?"

Before Aunt Helen could answer, Jessica and Robin burst through the front door onto the porch. Both girls were wearing long calico dresses and wide-brimmed fabric bonnets.

"Well," Jessica said, twirling around the porch. "What do you think?"

"I think you look like real pioneer women," Aunt Helen said brightly. "Where did you ever find those?"

"At the bottom of a trunk in a corner of the attic," Robin answered. "And we found two more. One could be altered to fit Stacey."

Aunt Helen reached for Jessica's wrinkled skirt. "They'll need some shaking out and ironing," she said. "And I'll tape up the hems so you don't trip."

"Come on, Elizabeth," Robin urged, "try on your dress!"

Elizabeth closed the photo album and followed the other girls upstairs. Later, when she had more time, she could give the photographs a closer look.

*   *   *

Even Aunt Helen dressed up for Gold Rush Day. Steven and Joe, however, refused to wear anything other than their usual jeans and T-shirts. "We're not going to look like geeks," Steven said.

"It's too late to start worrying about that," Jessica teased.

When they arrived in town almost everyone was dressed in costume. "Would you look at all the people!" Aunt Helen marveled as she parked the car.

A large banner was strung across Main Street reading WELCOME TO HOLTON GOLD RUSH DAY! in big gold letters. Colorful booths were set up along the street. The tiny local theater was showing a silent movie about the California gold rush of the mid-1800s. A big sign announced that Homer Bates, a local historian, would be giving a talk on the history of the area at one o'clock in the town hall.

"We're just in time for the history lecture!" Elizabeth said excitedly.

"Oh, please, Elizabeth!" Jessica groaned. "Have you forgotten this is summer vacation?"

"So?"

"So what do you think we're taking a vacation *from?* Things like history lectures!"

"Well, I'm going," Elizabeth said. "Does anyone else want to come along?"

Jessica, Stacey, and Robin shook their heads.

"I've got an idea," Aunt Helen said. "Why don't we all go our separate ways and meet back at the car in two hours?"

While the others headed for the souvenir and food booths, Elizabeth set off for the little white building that served as Holton's town hall.

Once inside, she settled onto a folding chair near the front of the lecture room. It was hot, and Elizabeth used her bonnet to fan herself while she waited for the lecture to begin. In a few minutes an old man with a cane made his way to a chair at the front of the room. He had a shiny bald head and a long, flowing white beard.

"For those of you who don't know me," he began in a gravelly voice, "I am Homer Bates." He wiped his forehead with a red handkerchief before continuing. "I was born right here in Holton some ninety-one years ago."

For the next hour, Homer Bates told tales about all the colorful characters of Holton, many of whose descendants still lived in the town. Elizabeth was sorry when the lecture ended.

As she was getting up from her seat, Homer Bates approached her and extended his hand. "It's always a pleasure to see young people interested in history," he said.

"I really enjoyed your lecture," Elizabeth told him.

"I've never seen you around these parts," the

old man said. "Are you one of the new people at The Lakeview Inn?"

"I'm Elizabeth Wakefield," Elizabeth answered. "My Aunt Helen just inherited the inn."

"Call me Homer," the old man said, smiling. "Your aunt's got her work cut out for her, I'll say that. It was a fine old house. When I was a boy, the place used to be the social center of the town. There were dances on the lawn every Friday night." Suddenly his smile faded. "Of course, you've already heard its tragic story."

"What story?"

"Why, the legend of The Lakeview Inn ghost, dear."

"I'd love to hear the story, if you have the time," Elizabeth said.

"Me? I've got all the time in the world!" Homer eased gently into a folding chair and motioned for Elizabeth to sit down also. "Mind you, every old house has a story or two attached to it," he cautioned. "But the legend of The Lakeview Inn ghost is particularly terrifying, because it may well be true. I can vouch for the truth of most of it myself. After all, I was right here, living in Holton, when it all started." He cleared his throat dramatically. "You *sure* you want to hear this?"

Elizabeth nodded. She loved a good story, even if it was a scary one!

Homer closed his eyes, as if trying to imagine

a time very long ago. "Many years ago, a young man by the name of . . . now, what *was* his name?" He paused and looked up at the ceiling. "William Cliff. Now I remember. Well, William fell in love with a beautiful girl who lived at the inn." He paused again. "Now, her name I don't rightly recall. But it seems the girl decided to marry another man. William was distraught. He couldn't bear the thought of life without her."

Homer widened his eyes. "The girl's parents prepared for a great wedding at the inn. All the townspeople were invited to attend. Only young William Cliff was not invited. But he came. As the ceremony got underway down by the shore of the lake, William snuck into the inn and climbed up to the bell tower."

The old man paused to clear his throat. "Just as the preacher asked, 'Does anyone here know any reason why these two should not be joined together in holy matrimony?' the bell in the tower began to ring. The young bride looked up to see her jilted lover draped over the railing of the bell tower."

"He killed himself?" Elizabeth cried in horror.

"No," Homer corrected her. "He had died of a broken heart at that very moment. The wedding was called off, and shortly afterward the inn was abandoned. The bell has never sounded since then. Legend says that The Lakeview Inn ghost, the ghost of young William Cliff, will haunt the inn until the bell is rung again to drive him out."

Elizabeth shuddered. "How horrible!"

Homer grinned. "Told you it was a gruesome tale. I hope I didn't scare you."

"Well, a little," Elizabeth admitted. "But I love ghost stories."

Homer stood slowly and leaned on his cane. "Well, I'd best be getting on. It was a pleasure meeting you, Elizabeth. Don't go having any nightmares on my account now, promise?"

Elizabeth laughed. "I promise," she said.

As she walked into the bright sunlight and scanned the crowd for Jessica, Elizabeth thought it would be silly to let an old man's ghost story bother her. What Homer had said about old houses was true—they all had ghost stories connected to them.

Elizabeth was wandering past booths selling cotton candy and "Gold Rush Burgers" when she noticed Aunt Helen's bright blue dress in the crowd.

"How was the lecture, dear?" Aunt Helen asked.

"Great. I learned all kinds of neat things about Holton."

"I'm glad you enjoyed it. You know, Elizabeth, I just learned there's a series of town meetings over the next several days, very important meetings. It seems a big developer wants to come into Holton. Now that I own The Lakeview Inn, I feel I have a responsibility to join the town's preservation effort. So I'd like to go to the meetings," Aunt Helen went on. "But I feel bad leaving you kids alone at the inn."

"Don't worry about us," Elizabeth reassured her. "We'll be fine."

Aunt Helen smiled gratefully. "I should be gone only a few hours each evening," she said.

Just then Elizabeth noticed Homer Bates in the crowd. "Aunt Helen?" she asked softly. "How much do you know about The Lakeview Inn ghost?"

"Well, we've never met personally," Aunt Helen joked. "But I did tell you the locals claim the inn is haunted. Why? Did you learn more at the lecture?"

Elizabeth shook her head. There was no point in retelling the story. "Homer Bates talked mostly about the gold-mining days."

Aunt Helen sighed. "Too bad. I'd like to get to know our ghost a little better!"

Thirteen

"Sorry I can't help out in the attic today," Jessica said sweetly.

"What do you mean?" Elizabeth demanded. "We didn't get any work done yesterday because of Gold Rush Day. And there's a lot to do before the family reunion."

"Today Aunt Helen assigned *me* an easy job," Jessica said. "She asked me to help her with the laundry."

"Since when do *you* like doing laundry?" Elizabeth asked with a laugh.

"Since the choice was between laundry and that creepy attic."

"Do you need help?" Robin asked hopefully.

"Oh, no, you don't, Robin," Elizabeth said firmly. "We have *got* to get some real work done up there!"

"I've done *plenty* of real work," Robin groaned.

As the other girls headed for the attic, Jessica set out for the laundry room, located behind the kitchen. The room contained two big, old-fashioned washing machines and a huge, noisy dryer.

Jessica sighed as she saw the gigantic piles of sheets collected in baskets. They were the sheets the girls had found packed away in the attic, and Aunt Helen wanted to see how they would look once they were laundered. Jessica realized it would take most of the day to complete the chore.

She loaded both the washers with sheets and dumped in a huge amount of detergent and bleach.

Later on, load after load kept coming out of the dryer, and Jessica quickly grew bored with folding sheets. She had to carry each folded load down a long corridor to get to the linen closet. Before long, Jessica was sweaty and very irritable.

"Elizabeth gets to have fun up in the attic while I have to work down here like a slave!" she muttered. "This is so unfair!"

Finally, the last load had been carried down the hall to the linen closet.

Jessica returned to the laundry room and glanced at the dryer. It was full of sheets.

"What?" Jessica groaned. "Where did those come from? I *did* all the sheets!"

There was nothing she could do but pull out this final load and carefully fold them. Before she carried them down the hall, Jessica looked closely inside each of the two washers and the dryer. All were completely empty.

She carried the sheets down the hall to the linen closet and put them away. Then she headed back to the laundry room to check one last time. As soon as she stepped into the laundry room, Jessica knew something was wrong.

Slowly, reluctantly, she turned her head to look at the dryer. It was full of hot, fluffy white sheets.

Jessica felt the hairs on the back of her neck stand up. She gulped and looked around her, afraid of what she might see.

But the laundry room was empty. Everything seemed perfectly normal.

"I checked the dryer," Jessica said out loud. The sound of her own voice gave her courage. "I *know* I checked the dryer!"

Jessica pulled out the sheets and carefully folded them. When she was done she took a few steps toward the linen closet, then turned and ran back to the laundry room.

"Caught you!" she cried as she burst through the door. But a quick glance reassured her there was no one there. And when she looked at the dryer, she saw that it was still empty.

Jessica breathed a sigh of relief. "I must have been dreaming," she said. "And I'm not coming back to this room," she added, raising her voice. *"So whoever you are, you can just stop this stupid game!"*

Jessica set off for the linen closet with the pile of sheets. She opened the door and began to set the sheets next to the others she had piled there.

But there was just one problem. The shelves were empty. The sheets were gone!

Don't panic, Jessica, she told herself sternly. *Try to be logical, like Elizabeth.*

"Elizabeth!" Jessica said suddenly. "Of course!" She nodded her head in sudden understanding. "Still trying to get revenge." She looked around, half expecting to see her twin skulking in a doorway. "Well, if that's the way you want it, Elizabeth, I'll show you that *two* can play this game!"

Elizabeth stretched out on her bed and eagerly picked up Alexandra's journal. Jessica was downstairs with Robin and Stacey, watching TV. Elizabeth had been looking for a perfect time to be alone with the diary, and this was it.

She opened the old book carefully and looked at the first page. Alexandra's handwriting was beautiful and very easy to read.

Dear Diary,

Today is August the ninth—my seventeenth birthday.

For my birthday I received this beautiful diary, which I shall faithfully keep from this day on.

Elizabeth turned the page.

August the tenth. Something odd happened today. I was sitting on the porch in the shade, doing my needlepoint and watching the swans on the lake, when who should come by but Will. I hadn't seen Will in some time, and he acted as if he hardly knew me. When I called hello he blushed, as though I had caught him in some mischief. Later I mentioned this to Annabelle, our cook, and she laughed and said she imagined young Mr. Will was fond of me. Naturally, this is a perfectly ridiculous idea, and I told Annabelle so, but she only laughed again and said, "Time will tell."

Elizabeth put the journal aside and got up to stretch. Then she headed for the bathroom and began to fill the tub with steaming hot water.

When the bath was full, Elizabeth went back to the bedroom. She opened the diary again and laid it open on the bed so she could read while she slipped out of her work clothes and into a terry-cloth robe.

August the eleventh. The weather was beautiful today. Because it was quite warm I decided to wear my new frock, which I do believe is very attractive. I naturally had no expectation that Will would be coming by—despite what Annabelle said when she saw me out on the porch. Nevertheless, he did walk by. He said he was going into town. He had happened, he said, to pick a rose that grew wild down by the mill, and he asked me if I would like to keep the flower. It was a very beautiful pink rose. I didn't want to hurt his feelings, so I accepted the flower.

Elizabeth turned the page of the diary and a flower, pressed and dried, fell out. She picked it up tenderly. The color had faded over the many years, but Elizabeth could see that it had once been a pink rose.

She carefully set the flower aside on the dresser and carried the diary down the hall to the bathroom. She set the book safely on a low bench beside the bathtub and stuck her toe into the water.

Elizabeth jumped back in surprise. Slowly, she bent down and stretched out her finger toward the water.

The water was no longer steaming hot. It was not even warm. In fact, it was freezing cold. And as Elizabeth's finger touched the surface of the water, she realized that there was a thin but firm coat of ice across the bathtub.

Fourteen

Elizabeth stormed out of the bathroom. "Jessica! I don't know how you did this, but it's *not* funny!" she shouted.

Elizabeth started to stomp down the stairs in search of her sister, who quickly appeared at the bottom of the stairs.

"What are you yelling about?" Jessica said, clearly annoyed.

"You know perfectly well what I'm yelling about, Jessica Wakefield," Elizabeth said angrily.

"No, I don't," Jessica replied.

Just as Elizabeth opened her mouth again, Aunt Helen appeared behind Jessica.

"What's the matter, girls?" Aunt Helen asked.

"It's Elizabeth. She's—" Jessica began.

Elizabeth cut her off quickly. "It's nothing,

Aunt Helen," she said, managing to smile. "I just wanted to talk to Jessica for a second."

"OK. Just try to keep it down. I have to call someone about the next town meeting. I'm beginning to get worried that the big developer will decide he wants The Lakeview Inn next."

Jessica climbed the stairs to join Elizabeth. "See how you upset her?" she said accusingly. "What was all that yelling about, anyway?"

"As if you didn't know!" Elizabeth hissed. "It was about your little bathtub trick, Jessica!"

Jessica looked suspiciously at her sister. "I have no idea what you're talking about, Elizabeth. But you'd better not be trying to trick me again."

"*Me* trick *you?*" Elizabeth said angrily. "You're the practical joker around here!"

"Oh, really? What about the laundry?"

"What *about* the laundry?"

"You know."

"I do not know," Elizabeth said, "but you *do* know about my bath!"

"And you know about the laundry!" Jessica said again.

"Oh, so you *admit* you know about my bath!" Elizabeth accused.

"I don't admit anything!"

"You just *did!*"

"Did not!"

"Did!"

"Which one of you is supposed to be the logical one?" Robin interjected.

Both twins spun around to see their cousin leaning against the banister at the bottom of the stairs.

"Robin!" Jessica said angrily. "I should have known! It was *you*, wasn't it?"

"And you probably sabotaged my bath, too!" Elizabeth added.

Robin held up her hands innocently. "I don't know what *either* of you is talking about."

"I'll just *bet* you don't," Jessica said sarcastically. "It all started with that stupid mask in the mirror!"

"I told you I had nothing to do with that!" Robin said.

"But you *are* responsible for the laundry today!"

Robin looked at Jessica in confusion. "*You're* the one who did the laundry."

"Don't play dumb with *me!*" Jessica cried.

"Or me either!" Elizabeth added.

"Children!" Aunt Helen's voice was angry and sharp.

All three girls froze. Aunt Helen was standing at the bottom of the stars, behind Robin.

"I am on the telephone," Aunt Helen said a

little more softly. "Now, I don't know what this fight is all about, but I do think you should continue it in your rooms."

Jessica and Robin headed for their bedrooms. Elizabeth returned to the bathroom with the intention of refilling the bath with hot water.

When she opened the bathroom door she gasped. The ice was gone, and the bathtub water was steaming hot.

"Steven!" Elizabeth groaned. "I should have known it was Steven all the time." She realized she would have to apologize to Jessica and Robin. But that could wait until after her bath. Right now she needed to calm down!

Later that night, Jessica agreed that Steven and Joe must have been behind the new round of pranks.

"What is *with* those two?" she asked wearily. "Don't they know when enough is enough?"

She crawled into her bed near the window and turned off her bedside light. Elizabeth climbed into her bed by the door, but left her own light on to read more of Alexandra's diary.

"Why are you reading that boring old thing?" Jessica asked with a yawn.

"It's not boring at all," Elizabeth said. "Even you might like it, Jess. It's really a love story."

"I'll bet they live happily ever after," Jessica mumbled as her eyes closed.

Elizabeth shook her head. "I have a feeling they don't."

When Elizabeth awoke, sunlight was streaming in through the window beside her bed. She moaned and rolled away from the light. *I should have closed the blinds last night*, she thought.

Suddenly, Elizabeth sat bolt upright in bed.

"J-J-Jessica!" she called. "J-Jessica, wake up!"

"Unh," Jessica moaned. "It's too early."

"Jessica, wake up this instant!" Elizabeth yelled.

Jessica sat up and stared at her sister. "What's the matter with you? Are you trying to scare me to death?"

Elizabeth took a deep breath. "Jessica, don't you see?"

"I don't see anything," Jessica grumbled. "I'm still asleep."

"Jess," Elizabeth said urgently. "I'm by the window!"

"Big deal. Go back to . . ." Jessica looked around at the room. She squinted and blinked, as if to check and make sure her eyes were working. "Don't I have the bed by the window?"

"Yes, Jessica, you do."

"Then . . . then, why are *you* in it?"

"I don't know." Elizabeth closed her eyes and

tried to remember the previous evening. "I definitely went to sleep in the bed by the door. I remember it clearly. And, see?" She pointed. "That's my robe on the chair by the door. That's where I left it when I got into bed."

"Did we walk in our sleep and somehow manage to change places?" Jessica wondered.

Elizabeth considered the idea for a moment. Then she reached under her pillow and drew out Alexandra's journal. She shook her head grimly. "I put this under my pillow when I went to sleep. It's still here."

"That means it wasn't *us* who moved. It was our *beds!*"

Elizabeth nodded her head.

"That's impossible!" Jessica protested. "Unless . . . is this some kind of trick?"

"Who could possibly have moved our beds clear across the room, with us in them, and not have woken us up?" Elizabeth demanded.

"Steven and Joe?" Jessica suggested lamely.

"They're not *that* strong!"

"Then who? Come on, Lizzie! You're the logical one. Who could have moved our beds?" Jessica's voice quivered with fear.

"Not even *men* could do this," Elizabeth said. "These beds are made of thick, heavy wood. Besides," she added, looking around the room, "this room is too small for the beds to have been pushed past each other."

"You're beginning to frighten me, Elizabeth."

Elizabeth nodded. "I'm beginning to frighten myself."

"Let's get out of here!"

"Robin's room," Elizabeth agreed. "Now!"

The two sisters leapt from their beds and ran to their cousins' room.

"I think you two are just making all this up," Robin said calmly after listening to the twins' tale.

"We are not!" Jessica responded hotly.

"There's something I haven't told you guys because I hoped it was just a silly old story," Elizabeth said seriously to her sister and cousins. "And if I tell you, you have to promise you won't tell Aunt Helen. She has enough to think about, and besides, she has all her money invested in fixing up the inn."

"What are you talking about, Elizabeth?" Jessica asked.

Elizabeth related the story of William Cliff and the ghost of The Lakeview Inn. As she spoke, the three faces gathered around her grew more and more grave.

"I can't believe you didn't tell us about this!" Robin said when Elizabeth finished her tale.

"I didn't think it was really important," Elizabeth said. "I mean, ghosts aren't real."

"If ghosts aren't real, who moved our beds in the middle of the night—with us in them?" Jessica demanded.

"It was the Lakeview Inn ghost!" Stacey cried dramatically.

Robin nodded. "The Lakeview Inn ghost! Here we've been *pretending* there was a ghost, and all the time there really *was* one."

"That was the face in the mirror!" Jessica cried. "And the creature that chased me in the attic. He's after us!"

"I really, really, really don't want to do this," Robin whined as the girls climbed the ladder to the attic.

"We have no choice," Elizabeth commented grimly. "Aunt Helen hinted we should get back to work today. What could we do? Tell her the inn is haunted?"

"I still really, really don't want to do this," Robin said.

"Me, neither," Stacey agreed.

The girls halfheartedly worked at clearing a path to the tower entrance. Whenever they heard a sound, they jumped.

When a few minutes later a deep male voice

said hello, all four girls froze until Jessica broke the tension.

"Hello, Bill," she said. "You startled us. We didn't hear you come up."

"I'm sorry if I scared you," Bill said apologetically. "I've met your sister, but I don't believe I've met these other two girls."

"This is Robin and Stacey," Jessica said. "They're our cousins." She turned to Robin and Stacey, who were eyeing Bill suspiciously. "Don't worry. Bill is one of the workers. He's the man who told me about the secret room."

Robin and Stacey smiled weakly.

"You all seem kind of jumpy," Bill commented.

"Yeah, we're worried about the Lakeview Inn ghost!" Stacey blurted.

Bill laughed heartily. "You girls don't really believe in ghosts, do you?"

"We . . . we're not exactly sure," Elizabeth said. "We heard a story about a man who died a long time ago in the bell tower. His ghost is supposed to haunt the inn."

"You know all about this inn, Bill," Jessica said. "Have you ever heard of it being haunted?"

"Well, there are a lot of stories," Bill answered. "It's hard to know which to believe and which not to believe. But I'll say this, young ladies—if I were you, I'd stay away from the bell tower."

The girls turned slowly to look at the cobweb-covered door to the bell tower. The four of them had been working to reach that door since Aunt Helen had given them the job of cleaning up the attic. And they were the only people the ghost seemed interested in bothering.

Elizabeth had a strange feeling Bill knew more than he had told them. She decided to get more answers from him. From the first time she had seen the bell tower, she sensed it held some terrible secret. But when she turned back to Bill, he had vanished.

"Where did he go?" Elizabeth asked.

The other girls tore their eyes away from the mysterious door. "I didn't see him leave," Jessica said.

"He must have gone back to work," Robin suggested.

"I'm going after him!" Elizabeth ran to the staircase, followed closely by the other three.

When they reached the front yard, the girls looked around at the group of workers who were setting ladders against the side of the inn and stirring big buckets of white paint.

"I don't see him anywhere," Jessica said.

"I think that man over there by the fence is the boss," Elizabeth said. She strode purposefully over to a large man dressed in a red plaid work shirt. "Excuse me, sir. Are you the foreman?"

The man smiled down at her. "Yes, ma'am. I'm Tom Hollyfield."

"I'm looking for one of your workers, and I don't see him around."

"Oh?" Mr. Hollyfield said. "Who would that be?"

"Bill."

"Bill?"

"Yes. I don't know his last name."

"Must be a mistake," Mr. Hollyfield said. "There's no one named Bill working here."

Fifteen

◇

"That does it! I want to go home!" Jessica flopped into the easy chair in the living room. "I want to go home and forget I ever even *heard* of The Lakeview Inn."

"Me, too!" Robin agreed. "First we scare each other, then we find out there's a *real* ghost, and now there's some creepy guy hanging around no one's ever heard of!"

"I'm going up to my room, and I'm not coming out except for dinner," Stacey announced.

"Me, too," Jessica said. "I don't care what Aunt Helen wants, I'm not going anywhere near that attic or that bell-tower door!"

"I'm going to call my mom tonight and tell her to get us out of here," Robin vowed.

"So am I," Jessica said. "All I want is to go to a nice, normal Unicorn meeting, hang out at the mall with my friends, and have a banana split at Caseys."

"You guys intend to leave Aunt Helen alone with a ghost and some weird man named Bill?" Elizabeth said.

"What do *you* want to do?" Jessica demanded.

"I think we should figure out how all of this fits together, and find a way to defeat this ghost. If that's what it really is."

"Fine, Elizabeth," Jessica said. "You go right ahead. You can call me in Sweet Valley and let me know how it all came out—*if* you can still call!"

Dinner was glum. Aunt Helen studied some official documents on local zoning laws while she ate. The four girls were silent, each worrying about the ghost and about Bill. Only Steven and Joe ate contentedly, helping themselves to seconds.

After dinner the girls gathered in the twins' room.

"I still think we should call our parents and have them take us home," Robin said.

"Even if we called them tonight, they wouldn't be able to come until tomorrow at the earliest," Elizabeth argued.

"They could send us money for bus tickets," Jessica proposed.

"That would take just as long," Elizabeth pointed out. "We would still have to spend the night."

"I know," Stacey said brightly. "We'll ask Aunt Helen for money for the bus."

"If we do that, we'll have to give Aunt Helen a good reason. We can't just say, 'Aunt Helen, your inn is haunted by the ghost of William Cliff, who died in your bell tower.'" Elizabeth said ruefully.

"She'd think we were all crazy," Jessica added.

"We're trapped!" Robin wailed.

"Let's try thinking about this logically," Elizabeth said.

"Since when are ghosts logical?" Jessica countered.

"Have you considered that maybe there *is* no ghost, and that Bill has been responsible for all that's happened?" Elizabeth asked. "Maybe he's an insane person who's escaped from an asylum."

Jessica groaned. "Is that supposed to make us feel better?"

Elizabeth shrugged. "I guess not."

"Maybe Bill is just a practical joker," Robin suggested. "Just one of the workers, with a twisted sense of humor."

"Mr. Hollyfield said he *wasn't* one of the workers," Elizabeth pointed out.

"Yes," Robin said, "but I have a very logical explanation for that! You asked about someone named Bill. But Bill is short for William. Maybe Mr. Hollyfield knows him as William, and he just didn't realize we were talking about the same man."

"Robin, you're brilliant!" Jessica said happily. "That's got to be it. He's just a practical joker and a normal workman, and there's no ghost at all, and—"

Jessica stopped talking when she saw Elizabeth's pale face.

"How could I have been so dumb?" Elizabeth whispered.

Jessica looked nervously at her sister. "What's the matter, Lizzie?"

"The photo album!" Elizabeth said suddenly. "Now I remember. Something about that picture seemed familiar. Where's that photo album?" Elizabeth tore through a dresser drawer as the other girls watched in silence.

"Here it is!" Elizabeth opened the album and flipped through the pages feverishly. "I know it's here, I know it's here!"

Suddenly she pulled a photograph from the album and stared at it until Jessica snatched the picture from her hand.

It was a photograph of a young woman and a young man. The young man seemed vaguely familiar.

"Read what's on the back," Elizabeth instructed.

Jessica turned the picture over and read the faint script. " 'Will and me. September nineteenth, 1920.' "

"Will," Elizabeth explained. "Alexandra's boyfriend. I should have realized it sooner."

"Realized what?" Jessica asked.

"Will. It's short for William. Bill is also short for William. Bill and Will and William Cliff, the Lakeview Inn ghost, are all the same person!"

Suddenly the window blew open and a tornadolike wind exploded in the room. The picture in Jessica's hand was torn away, as if an invisible human hand had plucked it from her grasp.

"No!" Elizabeth leapt desperately after the fluttering picture and snatched it from midair just before it reached the open window. She fell to the floor, clutching the photo. Abruptly the wind stopped and the window slammed shut.

"Look," Jessica said shakily. "Lizzie, look!"

Still dazed by her fall, Elizabeth slowly turned to follow Jessica's pointing finger. On the wall there were letters—horrible, bloodred letters that spelled the words:

Get out!

Then the letters faded and were gone. The wall returned to normal.

Elizabeth looked at the picture she had rescued. A young, pretty woman held hands with a young man who was smiling happily. Alexandra and Will—or Bill. They were standing in front of The Lakeview Inn. Above them rose the bell tower.

"We could have been killed!" Jessica whispered.

"We weren't hurt, though," Elizabeth said quietly.

"We *have* to tell Aunt Helen about this!" Robin cried.

"No!" Elizabeth said forcefully. "We can't tell Aunt Helen—"

Suddenly there was a knock at the door. "Girls? Are you in there?"

"Nobody say *anything*!" Elizabeth hissed. Then she called out brightly, "Yes, Aunt Helen. Come on in."

Aunt Helen opened the door. "I thought I heard pounding and someone screaming."

"Oh . . . um, that was, um, us," Elizabeth stammered.

"We were having a pillow fight," Jessica interrupted.

"A pillow fight?"

"Yes, but we're very sorry. Elizabeth made us stop." Jessica smiled at her sister.

"I'm glad that's all it was," Aunt Helen said. "You had me scared. My heart is still pounding!"

Elizabeth gave Jessica a meaningful look. "We're very sorry, Aunt Helen."

"Well, girls will be girls," Aunt Helen said with a chuckle. "I'm going to bed. I'll see you in the morning."

"Good night," the girls responded.

As soon as Aunt Helen had closed the door, Jessica sighed. "OK, I guess you're right, Elizabeth. We can't tell her."

"But what are we going to do?" Robin asked. "This stupid ghost is still hanging around."

"She's right," Jessica agreed. "He doesn't want us to go into the bell tower, and that's exactly what Aunt Helen wants us to do."

"The important question is, *why* doesn't he want us to go into the bell tower?" Elizabeth pointed out. "The old historian told me that when the bell in the tower was rung again, the ghost would be banished. Bill must be afraid that we'll ring the bell and send him away from Alexandra's home forever!"

The girls spent the night together in the twins' room. They took turns staying awake to watch for any new ghostly behavior, but nothing happened. By morning, when Aunt Helen called them down for breakfast, the whole horrible experience of the night before seemed vague and unreal.

"Good morning, girls," Aunt Helen said. "You're up late this morning. The boys have already eaten. They're down at the boathouse doing some painting."

"We were tired," Jessica said.

"Then what you need are some of my home-baked blueberry muffins," Aunt Helen said warmly. "They're in the oven right now and—"

She paused as the telephone rang in the parlor. "I'd better go get that," Aunt Helen said. "Would you girls mind taking the muffins out of the oven?"

"Sure," Elizabeth replied. As Aunt Helen headed for the parlor, Elizabeth found an oven mitt and opened the oven door.

Instantly, she slammed it shut.

"What's the matter, Elizabeth?" Jessica asked. "Did you burn yourself?"

Elizabeth gave her a queer look that made Jessica's spine tingle. "Take a look and tell me if I've gone crazy."

Jessica got up from her chair, followed closely by Robin and Stacey. Slowly, Elizabeth opened the oven door again. A dozen muffins sat in a muffin pan. And crawling over each muffin were dozens of tiny white wormlike things.

"Maggots!" Robin cried as Elizabeth slammed the oven door again. "Oh, gross! We learned about them in science class. They're disgusting!"

"Bill," Elizabeth said with a sigh.

"I guess he hasn't given up, has he?" Stacey said.

"We have to get rid of those muffins. Quick, before Aunt Helen comes back!" Elizabeth declared.

"Go ahead," Robin urged. "No one is stopping you."

Elizabeth grimaced. "Why do *I* have to do this?"

"Because you're so logical, we know *you* won't be afraid," Jessica said sweetly.

"Very funny." Elizabeth screwed up her courage and opened the oven door once again. Now the muffins looked perfectly normal. There were no maggots in sight. She pulled the muffin pan out of the oven and held it under Jessica's nose. "Anyone like to try a muffin?"

"I'd rather eat dirt," Robin announced.

"I'd rather eat one of Jessica's sandwiches," Stacey said.

Elizabeth carried the muffins to the garbage can and dumped them in, carefully hiding them with bits of trash. Just as she finished, Aunt Helen returned.

"That call was from the president of the town council. He's holding an emergency meeting this afternoon. I may be gone until quite late. But I'll leave the number of the town hall so you can reach me if there's any problem. And there's fried chicken and potato salad in the refrigerator for dinner." Aunt Helen looked at the four girls with concern. "Are you sure you'll be all right without me?"

"Don't worry about us," Elizabeth said with all the conviction she could muster. "We'll be fine."

Sixteen

"So how do you get rid of a ghost?" Elizabeth wondered as the girls settled on the landing by the lake. Jessica, Robin, and Stacey took off their shoes and let the warm lake water lap at their ankles.

"Remember that movie called *The Spooks?*" Stacey asked. "A family discovered their house was haunted, so they called in a woman who specialized in getting rid of ghosts."

"And how do you suggest we go about finding someone who specializes in ghost disposal?" Robin asked irritably.

"Look in the yellow pages," Stacey said.

Jessica giggled. "This isn't exactly like getting rid of termites, Stacey. We're talking major stuff here."

"The one thing I know is that we have to find

some way of getting rid of the ghost *other* than going into the bell tower!" Robin said strongly.

Stacey splashed her feet in the water. "Maybe we should call our parents and ask them."

"And say what?" Robin asked. " 'Hi, Mom and Dad. We're having a great time. By the way, do you have any helpful hints for getting rid of annoying household pests—roaches, rats, ghosts?' "

"You have a point," Stacey admitted.

Elizabeth twirled a strand of hair around her finger. "What we need is to come up with a plan of action based on what we already know about the ghost," she said thoughtfully.

"We know he has bizarre powers," Robin noted. "He can make writing appear on walls."

"And maggots on muffins," Stacey added.

"Do you think Aunt Helen would consider selling the inn?" Jessica asked. "I can see the ad now: 'For sale. One very old inn in very bad condition. Comes equipped with its own ghost.' "

"Seriously," Elizabeth pressed, "there's got to be an answer. I mean, aside from going up into the tower."

"This is one time that all the logic in the world won't help, Elizabeth," Jessica advised.

"Maybe we should talk to Steven and Joe," Robin suggested.

Jessica rolled her eyes. "They'll just laugh."

"You may be right, but we can use all the help we can get," Robin insisted as she stood up. "Come on, we can at least *try* talking to them. What can it hurt?"

"It's obvious you don't have a big brother, Robin," Jessica remarked.

Elizabeth rose and pulled her twin to her feet. "Come on, Jess. It's worth a try."

The girls found Steven and Joe in the boathouse. They'd been painting the interior walls for two days, but so far only one wall was completed.

"Boy, you guys are slow painters!" Stacey said as the girls stepped into the boathouse.

"We'll be done today. Besides, we're professionals," Steven protested. "Look at this quality workmanship!" he said, pointing to a windowsill still damp with white paint.

"Aunt Helen's workmen painted the entire parlor in a few hours," Jessica said as she settled onto a white bench.

"Yeah, but we work cheap!" Joe exclaimed. "Right?" he asked Steven, thrusting his paint-brush into the air like a sword.

Steven responded with a swipe of his own brush, and the boys began to leap about the room in a mock duel.

"You expect *them* to save us?" Jessica asked Robin, raising one eyebrow.

"Truce, Joe!" Steven called. He turned to Jessica, "Save you from what?"

"Well . . ." Robin began. "It's sort of a long story."

"Why don't you tell us the condensed version?" Joe said.

"Look, we've got a real problem," Jessica said. "Haven't you two noticed anything . . . well, *strange* about the inn?"

"Let's see," Steven said rubbing his chin thoughtfully. "When I took my shower this morning, there wasn't enough hot water."

Joe laughed. "And the room service is really unreliable," he added.

"This is *serious*, you guys!" Elizabeth said angrily.

Both boys stared at Elizabeth in surprise. "Elizabeth, what's wrong?" Steven asked. "You really *are* serious, aren't you?"

Elizabeth drew a deep breath. "I know this sounds crazy, but we think the inn is haunted."

Steven took one look at Joe, and both boys burst into gales of laughter. "You mean, by a ghost?" Steven asked when he'd composed himself at last.

"Of *course* by a ghost!" Stacey replied.

"And have you actually *seen* this ghost?" Joe asked.

All four girls nodded.

"What evidence do you have?" Steven asked.

"He put maggots in Aunt Helen's muffins this morning," Stacey said.

Steven pretended to be shocked. "Oh, *well* then!" he exclaimed. "Why didn't you *say* so?" He glanced over his shoulder at Joe. "Did you hear that, Joe? Maggots!"

"And he wrote a message on the bedroom wall," Robin added.

Steven set down his paintbrush. "Look, girls," he began, in the long-suffering tone the twins recognized as his big-brother voice. "We didn't mind helping you out during your little battle of the pranks. But don't try to fool *us* with some pathetic story about a ghost."

"Steven's right," Joe agreed. "You're out of your league, girls."

"But it's true!" Robin insisted.

"Please, you guys," Elizabeth said quietly. "We really need your help."

"This is the lamest set-up for a prank I've ever seen!" Steven reached for his brush and dipped it into a paint can. "Don't you agree, Joseph?"

"Extremely lame," Joe concurred.

Jessica rose from her seat on the bench and sighed. "I hate to say I told you so, Robin, but—"

"I know, I know," Robin said. "You told me so."

* * *

"I'm going to finish reading Alexandra's diary," Elizabeth announced when the girls returned to the inn.

"How can you read at a time like this?" Jessica said as she reached into the cookie jar.

"How can you eat at a time like this?" Elizabeth retorted.

Jessica bit into a chocolate-chip cookie. "I need my strength."

"Well, I'm hoping Alexandra's diary will give me some new ideas about how to deal with—" Elizabeth glanced over her shoulder to see if anyone was within earshot, "our *problem*."

Elizabeth took a cookie from the jar and headed upstairs to her bedroom. She climbed onto her bed and opened the diary to the page she'd marked with a bookmark. She skimmed over the now-familiar handwriting and paused when she came to the paragraph where she'd stopped reading.

For the rest of the afternoon, Elizabeth pored over every word of the diary. She was so engrossed, she didn't even notice when Jessica, Robin, and Stacey came into the room.

"Lizzie?" Jessica said quietly.

Elizabeth jumped. "Oh, it's you!" she said. "You scared me."

"Aunt Helen just left for the town meeting," Robin said. "And the boys went to see a movie."

Elizabeth set aside the diary and nodded grimly. "All right, then," she said firmly. "It's time."

"Time for what?" Jessica asked nervously.

"Time for us to solve the ghost problem," Elizabeth said firmly. "Someone has to do it, for Aunt Helen's sake."

"But how?" Robin asked.

"We have to do just what Bill doesn't want us to do," Elizabeth said with determination. "We have to go into the tower."

Suddenly the girls heard thunder growl in the distance.

Jessica groaned. "I was *afraid* you were going to say that!"

Seventeen

The inn seemed darker and creepier than ever as the four girls slowly walked to the attic stairs. Elizabeth clutched Alexandra's diary. When they reached the foot of the stairs, the girls stared up into the opening.

"Oh, no," Robin groaned. "Who turned off the lights up there?"

"I turned them off," Stacey said. "Dad always tells us to turn off the lights when we leave a room."

"Great, Stacey," Robin said. "I'm sure Dad will be very proud of you—if he ever sees you again!"

"Let's not panic," Elizabeth interrupted. "The light cord is right above the stairs."

"Who gets to go up there first and turn it

on?" Jessica asked, looking deliberately at Elizabeth.

"We could flip a coin," Elizabeth said hopefully.

Jessica thought for a moment. "Stacey, think of a number between one and ten, but don't tell anyone. Whoever guesses closest has to go."

"OK." Stacey nodded. "I'm ready."

"Elizabeth?" Jessica prompted.

"Um, eight."

"I choose two," Jessica said.

"Five?" Robin said hopefully.

"It was four," Stacey said.

"You were closest, Robin," Jessica said.

Robin gave her little sister a withering look. "Traitor!" She took a deep breath. Then, with quivering knees, she began to climb the staircase.

"Nice ghost," Robin called softly. "Nice little ghost. You don't want to hurt me. *I* wanted to go back to San Diego and leave you alone!" She hesitated when her head reached the opening. "I *still* want to go back to San Diego." Very, very slowly, she climbed the last two steps.

Elizabeth saw the light go on in the attic. "What do you see up there?" she called.

"Nothing!" Robin replied. "I have my eyes closed!"

"You have your eyes closed?" Jessica echoed.

"Yes! And I'm coming down now. All I was

supposed to do was turn on the light. You never said I had to look around." Robin quickly climbed back down the steps.

"Now we all have to go up," Elizabeth said.

"Who goes first?" Jessica asked.

"I've done my part," Robin said firmly.

"I'll go," Jessica said suddenly. She climbed halfway up the stairs and looked down at her sister. "That way it will be your turn to go first when we get to the bell tower!"

Jessica continued to climb the steps until her head was inside the attic. "It looks OK," she called down. "You guys better be right behind me!"

"We are," Elizabeth assured her.

Jessica climbed the last few steps to the attic floor. A moment later, Elizabeth reached her side. Robin and Stacey were not far behind.

"Well, we're here. Now what?" Robin asked.

"Now we move all that junk away from the tower door," Elizabeth said with determination.

The attic should have been familiar, but instead it seemed strange and threatening. The air was thick and heavy, and the shadows were darker than they had ever been. Boxes and crates, huge and grotesque, loomed over the girls.

Elizabeth put a hand out to the nearest crate. Suddenly a peal of thunder shook the house.

Through the windows Elizabeth saw a brilliant flash of lightning. A split second later the light in the attic flickered and went out.

The girls screamed. Elizabeth tried to stop herself, but then the lightning flashed again, sending blue light blazing through the attic.

In a flash of flickering brilliance, Elizabeth saw Jessica's face, her mouth wide open and her eyes black pools of shadow.

"Stop screaming!" Elizabeth cried at the top of her lungs. "It was just the lightning. It knocked the electricity out!"

The room was suddenly pitch black and silent. "Back to work," Elizabeth said, her voice ragged. At the next flash of lightning she shoved the crate and moved it several feet across the floor.

"We can't even see what we're doing!" Robin complained.

"Wait for the lightning flashes," Elizabeth advised.

"No way!" Robin shouted over the sound of the thunder. "We can't do it!"

"Lizzie's right!" Jessica yelled back. "We *have* to do it tonight! We'll never get up the nerve again!"

"I don't have the nerve now," Robin answered, but at the next flash of lightning, she threw her weight against a pile of boxes.

Elizabeth and Stacey shoved an old trunk and slowly moved it out of the path. But as soon as they moved on to another task, the trunk slid back into place.

Jessica squeezed through a narrow opening between the trunk and a crate to stand beside Elizabeth. "Here, I'll help you." She, Elizabeth, and Stacey pushed the trunk, and again slid it several feet to the side.

But when lightning once again illuminated the room, the girls watched the trunk slide back to its original position.

Elizabeth reached out to take Stacey's hand. She glanced over at her twin, who was too frightened to speak. Then Elizabeth saw Jessica's expression change. Her eyes narrowed and her chin jutted out.

"That does it!" Jessica announced. "I'm tired of being scared! I don't care what that old ghost does. We are *going* into that bell tower!"

"Come over here, Robin," Elizabeth called. "We have to stay together in one group. Let Bill try to stop us! We'll just keep moving forward!"

"But he'll cut off our way back!" Robin said.

"We're not going back," Jessica replied.

Working together now, the girls moved one box or trunk or piece of furniture at a time. As they moved each item, the ghost moved it to a spot behind the girls. Gradually, he succeeded in completely blocking their path back to the stairway.

"Let's move this chest of drawers next," Elizabeth said, pointing to a tall, heavy piece of furniture. As she did, the top drawer flew open.

An eerie blue light glowed from the drawer, and an old, white gown floated out, as if it were being pulled by invisible strings.

The girls fell back in fear as the gown began to jerk and wave like an insane puppet. Other drawers flew open and more garments rose to join the terrifying dance.

Suddenly one of the gowns dove at Jessica. She fell to the floor, her hands clasped over her head. A shirt, glowing a sickly green, flew at Robin, stretching out its arms to grab her.

A twirling, snakelike scarf slithered through the air toward Elizabeth. Then in a flash of lightning, Elizabeth saw the wicked, glittering blade of a sword slash through the air. Sliced in two, the scarf fell to the ground.

"Got you!" Stacey cried triumphantly. The next flash of lightning revealed her standing with her feet planted far apart, holding a knife more than a foot long in her hand.

Stacey turned and thrust the knife point at the shirt. Suddenly all the clothing fell to the floor around the girls.

"Hah!" Stacey yelled. "You don't want to fight anymore, now that I have my sword!"

"Stacey, what *is* that?" Robin cried.

"I found it when I dove into a box to hide," Stacey explained.

"It's one of those long knives soldiers used to put on the ends of their guns," Jessica said, getting up from the floor.

Elizabeth gasped. "A bayonet! Be careful with that thing!"

"Let's move that dresser before anything else comes out of it," Jessica said.

With all their might, the girls shoved the dresser aside. There, at last, was the door to the bell tower.

"We made it!" Jessica cried.

At that moment a huge flash of lightning illuminated the attic. Instinctively, the girls closed their eyes, and when they opened them again, they saw a blue fire snake along the ceiling overhead—a curving, brilliant string of electricity. They watched in terror as it sped along the ceiling and then crawled down to encircle the tower door.

"*No closer!*" a voice boomed. "*Get away! I warned you!*"

Elizabeth watched the blue fire snapping and crackling. Then she felt the hard surface of Alexandra's journal, which she had stuck into the waistband of her pants. She took a deep breath and stepped toward the door.

"Lizzie! Don't touch it!" Jessica shouted.

"We have to go through that door!" Elizabeth cried.

"But you'll be killed!"

"No," Elizabeth whispered. "No, I won't." Slowly, she reached out her hand. The electric current on her skin felt like a million crawling, tiny insects. Her fingers were only a fraction of an inch away from the doorknob.

And then the blue fire was gone. Elizabeth grasped the doorknob firmly. "We're almost done," she told Jessica wearily.

Elizabeth turned the stiff knob. With her heart hammering in her chest, she waited for a flash of lightning. When it came, she pulled the door open.

A blast of icy air struck her. She could make out a set of steps leading up to the tower landing. In the next flash of lightning, she could see the steps were crawling with spiders.

"Gross!" Jessica cried.

"What?" Robin demanded anxiously from several feet behind the twins.

"Spiders!" Jessica yelled. "Millions of them!"

"I don't think they're real," Elizabeth said cautiously.

"You don't? They look awfully real to me!"

"I don't think any of this is real," Elizabeth

continued. "I think it's all just an illusion created by the ghost."

"Great theory," Jessica said. "But what if you're wrong? They could be poisonous!" But, with a queasy, desperate grin, Jessica took a step forward. She put her foot down on the first step. Her shoe crunched on spiders. "They *sound* like real spiders."

Elizabeth moved beside her, crunching more spiders as she climbed up the stairs. "That's *enough*, Bill!" she shouted. "I don't care what you do to scare us, we're coming up there!"

Suddenly the spiders disappeared. Jessica sighed with relief. "You were right, Elizabeth! They weren't real."

"No," a voice said. "But *I* am!"

Eighteen

◇

"Bill!" Jessica cried.

Bill was standing on the landing at the top of the stairs. His skin glowed with a strange light.

"Bill, we have to come up there," Elizabeth said, her voice shaking slightly.

"I'm sorry, but I can't let you do that," Bill replied calmly. "I've tried every way I know to scare you away."

"Because you knew we were trying to reach the bell tower," Elizabeth stated.

"Yes. This tower is my home."

"Y-you live here?" Jessica stammered.

"I don't *live* anywhere."

"Then why don't you leave?" Elizabeth demanded.

"I can't," Bill said simply. Then his voice deepened. "I tried to get rid of you without hurting you, but you were very brave. Unfortunately, you leave me no choice. I must kill you!"

"No!" Jessica screamed.

"He won't," Elizabeth said quietly. "He won't hurt us."

"Don't be fools! Run away!" Bill howled, and the walls of the stairwell echoed with the sound.

Elizabeth stepped closer to the ghost. "No, you won't hurt us. You've frightened us, but you've always stopped short of hurting anyone. It was you who appeared in the two-way mirror, you who made my little ghost on the lake burst into flames. It was you who caused Jessica's laundry to disappear, and my bathwater to freeze, and you who switched our beds. And it was you who chased Jessica until she was ready to jump from the attic window."

Elizabeth moved closer, until she was standing on the landing with Bill. Over her head she could see the big brass bell. From it hung a frayed piece of rope. It was almost within reach!

"But you didn't let Jessica hurt herself," Elizabeth continued. "I remember I was desperately looking for the light cord when the light suddenly came on all by itself. You turned the light back on because you knew that would stop Jess from jumping."

Bill looked at Jessica and smiled faintly.

"And just now, Bill, when Stacey was waving that bayonet around in the dark, you stopped the flying clothes because you were afraid she might hurt someone."

Bill nodded slowly. "Life is more precious than you could ever know," he whispered. "Yet I have to stop you. *I must wait here.*"

"Wait for what?" Jessica asked.

"I am waiting for someone," Bill said. "She has been away a very long time, yet I feel certain that someday she will return. If I can see her face once more, just for one moment, then I can rest."

"Alexandra," Elizabeth whispered.

"Yes," Bill said sadly.

"She loved you," Elizabeth said gently.

Bill nodded slowly. "And I loved her."

"And when you heard she was to marry another man, you were so heartbroken you couldn't go on living," Elizabeth continued. "All for nothing." She shook her head sadly.

"What do you mean?" Bill demanded.

Elizabeth pulled the diary from her waistband. "This is Alexandra's diary. I've been reading it. Most of it is about you. About how much she loved you and wanted to marry you."

"But she married someone else!" Bill cried.

"No, Bill. She was being pressured by her father to marry a wealthy doctor from the next county. Alexandra could not make him change his mind. Finally she decided on a last, desperate measure."

Bill stood transfixed. "What are you saying?"

"It's here on the last page of her diary. I read it only an hour ago. I'll read it to you now." With trembling hands, Elizabeth opened the diary to the final page. " 'Tomorrow is to be my wedding day. But I will never wed any man save my darling Will. As the ceremony begins, before all those assembled and, most important, before my father, I will announce that Will is my one true love! After that, no other man will have me, and Father will have to agree to my wishes.'

"This part is . . . well, it's kind of written to you," Elizabeth explained. She felt tears well up in her eyes, and she brushed them away with the back of her sleeve.

"Read it," Bill said softly.

" 'After tomorrow, my beloved Will, I will be yours for all eternity.' " Elizabeth closed the diary. "That's the end."

The pale, eerie light had faded from his face, and suddenly Bill seemed no different from any other young man. He stood quietly for a long time. Elizabeth and Jessica waited with downcast eyes.

Finally, and sadly, Bill spoke. "I've waited here for her to return, and yet she never has."

"Bill," Elizabeth said softly, "Alexandra died a few months ago. She never married. I think she never returned because the memories were too painful for her."

Bill closed his eyes and bowed his head. "Then it is over. There is no more hope."

"There's *always* hope, Bill!" Jessica said through her tears.

"Not for me," Bill said. He pointed at the frayed rope that hung from the bell. "My time is done, my young friends. Will you ring the bell? Will you ring it for me?"

"Yes, Bill," Elizabeth whispered. "I'll do it for you." She crossed the floor and reached up to grab the rope. Jessica stood beside her and also reached up. With a last look at the ghost of the tragic young lover, they rang the bell.

There was a rush of air, warm and sweet, and a flash of light that made them blink. When they opened their eyes again, Bill was gone.

Nineteen

"I see Mom and Dad's van!" Jessica cried as she ran out onto the lawn to greet her parents.

"Jess! Wait!" Elizabeth called. "I need help with this sign!" As she watched her twin dash off, Elizabeth shook her head and went back to taping up the big posterboard sign the girls had made. WELCOME FAMILY! it read in big bold letters.

Robin finished tying a helium balloon to the porch railing. "Here, Elizabeth," she said. "I'll give you a hand."

A week had passed since Bill's disappearance, and the girls had never mentioned him since that fateful day. All week they had dusted and scrubbed and swept and tried to forget their terrible experience.

When the Wakefield van came to a stop, Elizabeth ran over to her parents. "Welcome to the new, improved Lakeview Inn," she said. "What do you think?"

"It's beautiful!" Mrs. Wakefield said.

"Looks great," Mr. Wakefield agreed as he pulled a suitcase from the van.

"This is the *after* picture," Jessica reminded him. "You didn't get to see the *before!*"

As they walked toward the porch, Aunt Helen came bursting through the front door. "Ned! Alice!" she cried. "It's so wonderful to have you here! You're the first ones to arrive for the reunion."

Aunt Helen led Mr. and Mrs. Wakefield into the parlor. "Why, it's gorgeous!" Mrs. Wakefield exclaimed.

Aunt Helen gazed proudly at the immaculate, sunlit parlor. The sheets had been pulled off the antique furnishings. The cobwebs and dust had vanished. And on every table sat a vase of fresh flowers.

"Wait until you see the attic!" Robin said.

"The attic?" Mr. Wakefield repeated in surprise.

"The girls did an amazing job of cleaning it," Aunt Helen said gratefully. "When they volunteered to help me, I don't think they realized what they were getting into."

"You can say *that* again!" Jessica whispered to Elizabeth.

"And don't forget the boathouse," Steven called, coming into the parlor with a sandwich.

"There you are!" Mrs. Wakefield cried. "Come here and give me a hug, Steven!"

"I hope the boys were on their best behavior," Mr. Wakefield said to Aunt Helen with a wink.

"They were wonderful," Aunt Helen replied. "Perfect angels!"

"They didn't pull any practical jokes on you?" Mr. Wakefield asked the girls.

Jessica looked at Steven. "They were perfect angels!" she repeated with a laugh.

By evening, the entire family had arrived at the inn. A few members of the Holton town council, as well as Homer Bates, joined them. Mr. Wakefield and Stacey and Robin's father had set up a big barbecue by the edge of the lake, where they were cooking hamburgers, chicken, and steaks. Aunt Helen had baked biscuits and blueberry pies.

By the time night fell, the girls were so full that they could do nothing but collapse under a tall tree. They were giggling and laughing when something black and very creepy dropped out of the tree, straight into Jessica's lap.

Jessica looked down calmly and plucked the rubber spider from her lap.

"What is it?" Elizabeth asked.

"Oh, just a rubber spider." Jessica peered up into the dark branches of the tree. "Steven and Joe are up there, attempting another pathetic practical joke."

Steven and Joe jumped to the ground.

"Not even one little scream!" Steven complained.

"I can't believe it!" Joe cried.

"Here." Jessica threw the spider back to Steven. "We're not afraid of spiders."

"Or ghosts," Robin added.

"Or flying shirts!" Stacey chimed in.

"Flying shirts?" Steven echoed in confusion. "Come on, Joe. These girls are too weird!"

When the boys had gone, the girls relaxed and gazed out over the moonlit lake.

"I guess from now on we'll be pretty hard to scare," Jessica commented. "Poor Steven and Joe." She turned to Elizabeth, but her twin was staring intently into the dark shadows under the trees that bordered the lake.

"Look!" Elizabeth cried, pointing.

Jessica followed the direction of Elizabeth's finger. There in the shadows she saw the faint glowing shape of a young man.

"Bill," Jessica murmured.

Suddenly a second figure seemed to materialize. It was a beautiful young woman, dressed in a lacy, flowing white dress.

"Alexandra," Elizabeth whispered. "Just the way she looked when she was young!"

The four girls watched as the two spirits joined hands and walked out over the water to the center of the lake. They stood together, hand in hand, then turned and slowly waved farewell to the girls. Finally they stepped into the rippling, silvery moonlight and were gone.

"They're together at last," Robin said with a sigh.

When Jessica caught her breath, she turned to Elizabeth. "All right, Lizzie," she said. "Explain *that* logically!"

"Oh, that's easy," Elizabeth said, smiling wistfully. "True love is very, very logical."

"...hope," said The Oldest in the Land. Tonge...

...was a beautiful young woman, dressed in
a long, flowing white dress.

"...Cleopatra," Elizabeth whispered. "Just the
way she looked when she was young."

...the four girls watched as the two ghosts
joined hands and walked out over the water to
the center of the lake. They stood together, hand
in hand, then turned and slowly waved farewell
to the girls. Finally they stepped into the rippling
silvery moonlight and were gone...

"...they're together at last," Robin said with a
sigh.

...Elizabeth ...jumped up into bed, cheerful, and turned
to Elizabeth. "All right, Lizzie," she said. "Explain
that to me."

"Oh, that's easy," Elizabeth said, smiling.
"Why? True love is very, very powerful."

We hope you enjoyed reading this book. If you would like to receive further information about available titles in the Bantam series, just write to the address below, with your name and address: Kim Prior, Bantam Books, 61–63 Uxbridge Road, Ealing, London W5 5SA.

If you live in Australia or New Zealand and would like more information about the series, please write to:

Sally Porter
Transworld Publishers
(Australia) Pty Ltd
15–23 Helles Avenue
Moorebank
NSW 2170
AUSTRALIA

Kiri Martin
Transworld Publishers (NZ) Ltd
3 William Pickering Drive
Albany
Auckland
NEW ZEALAND

All Bantam and Young Adult books are available at your bookshop or newsagent, or can be ordered at the following address: Corgi/Bantam Books, Cash Sales Department, PO Box 11, Falmouth, Cornwall, TR10 9EN.

Please list the title(s) you would like, and send together with a cheque or postal order to cover the cost of the book(s) plus postage and packing charges of £1.00 for one book, £1.50 for two books, and an additional 30p for each subsequent book ordered to a maximum of £3.00 for seven or more books.

(The above applies only to readers in the UK, and BFPO)

Overseas customers (including Eire), please allow £2.00 for postage and packing for the first book, an additional £1.00 for a second book, and 50p for each subsequent title ordered.

Created by Francine Pascal

Jessica and Elizabeth Wakefield have had lots of adventures in *Sweet Valley High* and *Sweet Valley Twins* . . .

Now read about the twins at age seven! All the fun that comes with being seven is part of *Sweet Valley Kids*. Read them all!

SWEET VALLEY HIGH

The top-selling teenage series starring identical twins Jessica and Elizabeth Wakefield and all their friends at Sweet Valley High. One new title every month!

SWEET VALLEY SUPER STARS

SWEET VALLEY SUPER EDITIONS

SWEET VALLEY MAGNA EDITIONS.

THE SADDLE CLUB

Bonnie Bryant

Share the thrills and spills of three girls drawn together
by their special love of horses in this adventurous series.

1. HORSE CRAZY
2. HORSE SHY
3. HORSE SENSE
4. HORSE POWER
5. TRAIL MATES
6. DUDE RANCH
7. HORSE PLAY
8. HORSE SHOW
9. HOOF BEAT
10. RIDING CAMP
11. HORSE WISE
12. RODEO RIDER
13. STARLIGHT CHRISTMAS
14. SEA HORSE
15. TEAM PLAY
16. HORSE GAMES
17. HORSENAPPED
18. PACK TRIP
19. STAR RIDER
20. SNOW RIDE
21. RACE HORSE
22. FOX HUNT

Forthcoming:

23. HORSE TROUBLE
24. GHOST RIDER